GUVERNIA PARADISE

Ismail Serinken

True Potential
REACH THE WORLD

GUVERNIA PARADISE

Cover and Interior Page design by True Potential, Inc.

ISBN: 978-1-943852-63-5 (paperback)
ISBN: 978-1-943852-64-2 (ebook)

Library of Congress Control Number: 2017945247

True Potential, Inc.
PO Box 904, Travelers Rest, SC 29690
www.truepotentialmedia.com

Printed in the United States of America.

CONTENTS

GUVERNIA PARADISE

PROLOGUE

BEHIND EVERY LEGEND IS AN ELEMENT OF TRUTH.

As time goes by, extraordinary events from the past slowly lose their images, then their voices and finally their memories.

Neither the power of time nor forgetful minds could erase such events from the memories of mankind. Hidden in these memories are the secrets of where we really come from and who we truly are, and a parallel, mythical world named Guvernia.

Once thought to be just a myth, this story is of the immortal Guvernians and a mortal man who desperately pursued immortality.

We are separated from the Guvernians by an invisible wall of energy called Quadronia.

Like a pleasant breeze in the wind, from time to time, we feel their existence in our dreams, but we are invisible to one another. We are two different races who share a common world. We live in a mortal world full of pain and misery, while they live in a utopian society. Unfortunately, this perfect society was shattered when an earthquake rippled through the Sahara Desert, causing an energy shift that divided the Quadronia Wall.

GUVERNIA PARADISE

CHAPTER I — DREAM

BEADS OF SWEAT SLID DOWN HIS FOREHEAD AS he slowly straightened up in his bed and took a deep breath.

"When?" he whispered hopelessly, but paused as if waiting for a reply.

Glancing at the rainbow beams of light reflecting from the chandelier onto his bedroom wall, he sighed. How he craved to see the vivid colours from his dream once more.

But they weren't there. Everything was again a familiar mediocre.

The deep quiet that rang in his ears gave him the same answer he wished he didn't receive, "You have to wait."

He did not have the strength or the patience to endure it any longer. His heart was bitter like a child who refused to be consoled, and lasted long after the dream. To him, it was not just a dream but also a distant reality.

Jack Lawrence was a young, talented journalist at the top of his profession.

As a child, Jack had a penchant for searching for the truth, and his curiosity only grew as he matured into adulthood, giving him the drive required to become a talented journalist. For Jack, everything had to have a practical explanation and a satisfying answer.

"My boy, every question has an answer, but only if you look in the right place. Remember, life is like a game of hide and seek. The answers are just waiting to be found." These are the words his father often said to him and are the same words he founded his entire career upon. Now in his late twenties, Jack had travelled up the ranks in the newsroom because of his tenacious work ethic.

However, Jack's obsession lies in something else—finding the origin of those strange dreams that continue to haunt him.

His ruthless search had begun to shadow all of his other successes and had turned him into an introvert. Ever since waking up from that dream, it was always in the back of his mind. He believed he had evidence that proved it was anything but a dream. He had a deep indescribable longing in his heart for the things he had seen, but his logic told him that he couldn't feel longing for something that didn't exist. But this longing, instead of fading, only grew more intensely.

Just before waking up, he had seen a face among those unfamiliar colours. A heavenly voice spoke to him and told him to wait. This voice was his greatest evidence, always reminding him that this was more than a dream.

He would drift to sleep in the hopes of seeing the colours and hearing the voice, and though waking up with disappointment, he never thought of giving up. He had waited for years, and this longing had now become his life's purpose.

Jack was a workaholic. He loved his job with a passion—some of his colleagues mockingly told him he was married to the job.

His introverted personality and existential views gave him an intriguing air of character, and although he attracted many women, he rarely showed interest. He would rather dedicate his time uncovering the truth. His boss, Arnold, thought he was an outstanding employee and would often praise him. Jack was also popular with the readership, with people hanging on his every word. His findings were well trusted by the community and so he was usually given the task of researching breaking news. This meant Jack had plenty of rivals in the newsroom as well as at other companies.

Jack was aware of this, but finding the truth was top priority, and he would risk anything in the pursuit of it. Anything else was unnecessary and distracting.

What Jack knew well but others never seemed to realise was that things were never actually what they appeared to be. It was just a matter of finding the clues.

Jack Lawrence didn't overlook many things. He was a professional in finding the crucial information hidden in the unimportant details. He was, however, annoyed that the clues he had been searching for in regards to his dreams were nowhere to be found. He just had to wait, and he hated it.

He would often escape reality and drift into the thoughts of those dreams, hoping to find the answers he had been searching for. Though some may call him mad for eschewing reality like this, he enjoyed retreating into his deepest thoughts. His 'madness' helped him get closer to the dream he longed to understand.

***

Recently Jack found himself thinking of his father and of his death. During that period of loss, his deep pain first led him to rebellion and then caused him to question if the enemy whom had so cruelly stolen his father from him would ever be defeated. Graham Lawrence had been lost at sea, buried in the depths of the ocean and never found. Jack wanted to defeat this metaphysical enemy.

Jack was seventeen when he lost his father and did not take it well by any means. Many surrounding the family thought he dealt with his father's passing coldly, isolating himself to the point of neglecting his sickly mother. But this was not because he was a cold-hearted man. He just never came to terms with the concept of death.

During this quiet and despairing period, Jack had thought deeply about life and death. Everyone thought death was a part of the natural life cycle. But Jack was not so easily convinced. *Could death be reversed? Is it merely a curable disease?*

It was on the night of his father's passing that he first had that mysterious, life-altering dream. After all these years, the only scene that remained from the dream, the scene he desperately didn't want to forget, was that sweet, innocent voice that told him to wait. After waking up, the mind that he so trusted, along with his senses, worked much differently.

It seemed his perception of reality had changed. The outside world was different, as if it had lost its brilliance and become dreary and colourless. Nothing could, after all, be compared to the colours he saw in his dream.

Since that day, Jack Lawrence had been struggling to reconcile his internal and external world. On the inside, he felt he was a part of a world without limits, but on the outside, he felt as though there were boundaries stopping him. He knew he could never be free until those walls were broken, and he was ready to do anything—no matter what it took.

Many surrounding the family thought he dealt with his father's passing coldly, isolating himself to the point of neglecting his sickly mother.

After the new enlightenment and change in his senses, Jack started to analyse death. Everyone ran away from it, but in the end, it always caught up to people. Humans had, throughout all of time, tried to fight it, but in the end gave up and welcomed it.

His new sense of limitlessness told him the invisible enemy of mortality could be beaten. He believed death could be cured. But now he found himself in a twisted game of hide and seek.

Jack's dreams had told him where the cure was, but he knew he had to sit and wait. When the time was right, it would reveal itself.

***

Jack sat on his balcony one evening, drinking his coffee and watching the sunset. The sprawling city laid out in front of him and the fading sunlight always calmed him. He regularly spent his nights sitting outside watching the world go by. Suddenly, the roaring sirens of an ambulance broke the calm. Jack cringed as he was reminded of the fleeting nature of life and its fragility.

Then an image caught Jack's attention: a little boy, with his distended stomach and limp arms, was slowly dying. Jack was horrified.

He made his way inside and turned on the television to the nightly news. Sitting down on his couch, he heard the sirens once again.

"When?" His hand resting on his forehead in exasperation, he felt helpless and disparaged.

Deciding it was probably time to go to bed, Jack climbed under the covers and began to get comfortable. As he did so, the news changed to a story about the crisis in

Africa. For a second he felt like turning off the television, but the topic caught his attention.

He climbed out of bed and sat back down on his couch. The program was called *Dark Continent's Dark Fate*.

The program said that after extensive research, scientists had reached the conclusion humankind originated from the continent of Africa. It also mentioned that scientists were unsure of how the population had become so widespread despite being so few in number.

It talked about Africa's dark fate: the droughts, the children dying from starvation, and how dictators were committing genocide.

Then an image caught Jack's attention: a little boy, with his distended stomach and limp arms, was slowly dying. Jack was horrified. When he looked at the poor child, he was reminded of his own helplessness.

"No!" he said, taking choppy breaths. "No, this isn't fair." Jack exploded into a rage but then into fits of sobbing until he fell asleep.

That night he dreamed about Africa. In his dream, he found himself standing in the middle of an endless desert, stretching on into eternity. Suddenly, a huge tremor shook the ground, followed by a tsunami of sand on the horizon. The sandstorm rumbled on and on, and then everything eventually settled. Jack could now see that among the sands was a city, surrounded by a wall made of blue lights. Directly in front of the main gate stood a mysterious, yet familiar child. Jack felt as though he knew the boy. His wavy hair shone under the sun like gold and shook in divine magnificence. He took sand from the ground and scattered it into the air, letting it dissipate in the wind. The child with the face as bright as the sun laughed in a unique voice as he looked at the sand, raining like gold dust. He turned to Jack and looked at him thoughtfully, smiling all the while. The look on his face seemed to tell Jack, "The time has come."

Jack was in shock when he woke up. This dream was definitely connected to the one he had dreamt ten years ago. It felt like a huge weight had been lifted off his shoulders. In is heart existed such an unexplainable excitement; he wanted to shout in joy.

Jack entered his office building, realising he could no longer continue living under the oppression of these limitations. If last night's dream was anything to go by, it was time to take action.

"Jack!" Arnold called from his office door. "Are you alright? You seem... out of sorts."

"I'm fine. In fact, better than I have ever been before."

"Who is she? The girl? There must be someone."

"No, no," Jack chuckled. "I'm not in love. I'm just feeling like I'm due for a holiday—an adventure, maybe."

"Jack, I don't get you, but I'm glad you're happy. Happy people are efficient people, after all," Arnold said before exploding into his high-pitched laughter.

Jack let out a polite laugh, and then there was a second of silence. In his heart he doubted, at first, if he should share with his boss what had been going on, but then the words slipped out of his mouth as if they had made their own decision. "You know, Arnold, for years I have been searching for answers to something very specific."

"Jack, you're always asking questions and following up leads. It's your job," he replied, laughing again.

After a pause, Arnold looked at him. "But what is it then exactly?"

Jack took a deep breath. "I don't know how to explain it. It's kind of a complicated situation. It seems crazy even to me, but I trust my instincts, and they are telling me there are answers out there. I believe last night, after many years, I had a revelation. I had fallen asleep without realising it and had quite the peculiar dream. I was in a vast African desert when an earthquake hit, followed by a sandstorm. When the storm settled and my vision cleared, I saw a city rising from the sand. A child with hair that shone like gold stood in front of the entrance to the city. The child would pick up the sand and scatter it in the air. He then turned and stared at me with curiosity. For some reason, his face was familiar, and he seemed to be beckoning me towards him. Then I woke up and felt like I had been born again."

Suddenly, a huge tremor shook the ground, followed by a tsunami of sand on the horizon. The sandstorm rumbled on and on, and then everything eventually settled. Jack could now see that among the sands was a city, surrounded by a wall made of blue lights.

Jack's boss looked at him with a baffled expression. "Jack, that definitely is an interesting dream," he said, shaking his head. "Honestly, I don't know how to respond. Some people believe dreams have a meaning or a message."

"I know the meaning," Jack said.

"Jack, I need to go," Arnold said, with a note of concern in his voice. "I have an appointment waiting for me. We can continue our conversation later. As you know, we have a busy day waiting for us, so it's time to concentrate on our work and return to the real world."

But to Jack, he was in the real world.

GUVERNIA PARADISE

CHAPTER II — EARTHQUAKE

THE PHONE RANG SOMETIME BEFORE DAWN. When Jack opened his eyes, it was still dark, and he saw that the time was only 3:45 am. *Who would call me at this time?*

His mother was the first person who came to mind. Caroline was sickly and had been confined to a wheelchair after a traffic accident three years prior. She often needed Jack's support, both physically and emotionally. But his mother hadn't called. It was Arnold.

"Jack," Arnold said immediately then went silent for a second. "Earlier this morning, a massive earthquake hit the Sahara Desert, which caused an unforeseen sandstorm. NASA's satellites have confirmed it. But the strange thing is Africa isn't near any fault lines. Sources close to NASA say they detected an immeasurable energy coming from the epicentre. They are thinking the cracking and breaking of the crust caused by the earthquake led to an energy field emanating from the heat of lava—all of which completely contradicts their geological understanding of the area."

While his boss Arnold continued to speak, Jack had already disengaged from the conversation. He was thinking about the dream he had seen—the huge tremor in the desert, the sandstorm that followed it, and then the city that rose from among the sands.

"Jack, are you there?" Arnold asked. "Are you listening? This situation is really strange, don't you think?"

Jack quickly tried to regain composure, "Yes, very."

"Jack, listen. NASA is talking about a threat on the climate and the planet. National Security is now involved, and they're assembling a team to go and investigate. They want you on it."

"Me? Why? I thought they hated getting the press involved."

"No, they don't want you there as a reporter. They think your talent for investigative journalism will be helpful. In fact, you'll be one of the only people there who isn't a scientist or a soldier. It makes me wonder how serious the situation really is. They need you there, so nothing is overlooked."

Jack interrupted his boss, "Arnold, remember the dream I told you about yesterday morning? Do you think this is a coincidence?"

Arnold was quiet for a second. "I don't know, Jack," he said. "You know me well. I'm a realist."

"Well then, what type of reality is this? An earthquake in Africa happens one day after my dream, and now I'm being asked by the National Security to join a team going there?" Jack asked.

"I don't know. But you have to start packing because they're coming to pick you up in an hour. We may not be able to communicate for a few days. Call me at first chance and inform me of things. Don't forget, you still work for me," he finished, laughing, then hung up.

Jack was left to ponder the enormity of the situation. The time for waiting was over. The hunt was about to begin.

He opened his wardrobe and then packed his suitcase, neatly folding his clothes. He inherited this trait from his mother. Caroline gave great importance to maintaining order. Jack now remembered his mother and wondered if he should call. He quickly wrote her a message. "Mother, I am going on an overseas trip for a short time. I'll call you when I can."

A few minutes later, he heard a knock on his door. He opened the door to two men representing National Security, one of which spoke, "Jack Lawrence?"

Jack nodded.

The men took Jack to a military base one hour away, where he was then rushed into a waiting helicopter. He was flown to a larger base, where he a uniformed officer greeted him.

"Mr. Lawrence, I'm Colonel McKenzie. Welcome to our base. I've been following your work for a while. We apologise for calling upon you on such short notice, but I am sure you can appreciate the interest and urgency of this unexpected situation."

Nodding respectfully, Jack replied, "No problem."

They descended to a classified sector seven floors below the ground. As Jack inspected his surroundings carefully, he realised there was a serious security wall around the building. The Colonel, who eyed him from her peripheral, smiled at the visitor's intrigue.

They entered a hallway filled with people. An active argument was taking place, but Jack's eyes were quickly drawn to the images on the large screen mounted on the far wall. In the centre of the hurricane was a grey area that resembled an eye, holding what looked to be a blue light. Jack quickly realised these were satellite images from the sandstorm in the Sahara Desert.

Jack heard someone say, "There is something wrong here."

Unable to look away from the screen, Jack took a seat and continued to watch the broadcast of the sandstorm.

He then asked, "Can I say something?" No one heard him over the uproar taking place in the room.

Coughing loudly, he raised his voice. "Excuse me," he said.

Colonel McKenzie, who realised what he was trying to do, rose to her feet. "Excuse me!" Immediately, the hall fell silent. "This is Jack Lawrence. I am sure many of you are aware of who he is and his work as an investigative journalist. He has something he wishes to say."

With great interest, the occupants of the room rested their eyes on Jack.

"That thing, that shining light is actually not there, you do realise," Jack said. "The energy of magma is not stable. The other light that represents the energy of the storm is always blinking, but the blue light is moving in a motion fully independent from that of the powerful storm. The light is like a picture that has been copied and then pasted on the screen. There's something wrong there. The light is there, but also it is not."

**

General Watson, an important member of the National Security Committee, rose to his feet. In his full, powerful voice, "The thing that worries us is this," he said. "We cannot deal with an enemy who is there and also not there, and we certainly cannot deal with an enemy whose existence hasn't been proven. After our initial analysis, National Security has increased the situation to a code red emergency, meaning

In the centre of the hurricane was a grey area that resembled an eye, holding what looked to be a blue light.

we will also have to inform and update our allies. This situation does not just threaten us. It may threaten the whole planet."

"Excuse me, General," Jack said. "We do not know exactly what this is, but I think it's safe to say it will not affect our climate. Its very existence is up for debate."

"Sir, Mr. Lawrence may have a point," the Colonel interjected. "We can't even measure the force of the energy wall on the screen. According to our data, this energy wall isn't even from this world. As of this moment, the energy wall does not pose any immediate threat."

After the Colonel finished speaking, the room once again settled into an unsettling silence. For a short time, everyone looked at the mysterious light on screen. *What on earth was it?*

The General spoke, breaking the silence with firm assurance. "We have to get on the ground and know what we are dealing with. We leave tonight."

GUVERNIA PARADISE

CHAPTER III — AN OLD LEGEND

AT MIDNIGHT, THE TEAM BOARDED A MILITARY plane headed to an aircraft-carrier in the Mediterranean Sea just off the coast of Libya.

Around the world, news reports were emerging of the damage the sandstorm had caused. As a precaution, local authorities issued warnings of destructive flooding in Europe.

Jack eavesdropped on the conversation between Colonel McKenzie and General Watson, who sat in front of him. "General, satellite data shows visibility in the area is virtually zero due to the severe sandstorm. I think our flight and landing may be a challenge."

Laughing brashly, "Not to fear, Colonel. These new advanced military planes have been christened the 'Bats' because of their special radar systems. These babies can fly blindly through anything."

"However, our flight path intercepts with the eye of the storm, proving too dangerous to continue our journey in the air. We are forced to complete it by foot, adding two days to our schedule.

"Just North of the energy wall, we have determined a safe point. As you know, for security's sake, there are some risks involved that remain classified. However, our headquarters have started preparing the equipment should our mission be compromised. By the time we get there, the compound will be established and ready for us to begin work immediately. We cannot afford to waste any time. I don't have any friendly feelings for a foreign energy that suddenly pops out of nowhere."

The secrecy of the risks had captured Jack's attention, but he knew from prior experience to be suspicious of any statements made by soldiers.

He opened his laptop to research more about Africa and its history of earthquakes. While inspecting a seismic map of the continent, he saw that the epicentre was nowhere near any fault lines.

He considered artificial seismic activity, but he felt like he shouldn't worry himself thinking about it. Jack was not interested much in the reason of the earthquake, but whether the journey would or would not lead him to the place he so desperately wanted to reach.

Jack started researching the geological makeup of Africa. A number of geologists had suggested the Sahara and Namibia deserts had once been blanketed by thick forestry and expansive water basins. But as a result of severe evaporation and high temperatures, nothing was left but barren land. Admittedly, there was contention in the scientific community if this was indeed the case. But still to this day, no concrete evidence had proven either theory of the disappearing water basins and dried landscape. *Maybe it was an earthquake?* Jack wondered.

While Jack continued his research, he found other information that supported his hypothesis. Many fossils belonging to marine creatures had been found in the deserts' sediment, some distance from the water basins. It was certain the whole area had once been underwater.

Jack scratched his head, but he needed to rest. He fell asleep while flying over the Atlantic Ocean on his way to the Mediterranean. Tomorrow will bring another opportunity to investigate.

The dream returned. Though under the burning African sun, the child did not even seem to be affected; he looked at Jack and smiled. Jack heard the unique voice of the child echoing through the wind's breeze—the same voice that had consumed his mind for years.

"Jack, come here," the voice said. When Jack lifted his head, he saw the sky had been filled with sand. But where the child stood, the sky was clear and blue. Jack then glimpsed a technicolour halo of light completely surrounding the child. He wanted to approach the child, but he was jarred awake when the airplane entered a pocket of rough turbulence. The airplane teetered dangerously.

They were above the Mediterranean when Jack looked out of his window and all he could see was a brown dust cloud. The pilot quickly started to ascend in hopes that the dust cloud was thinner higher up. But in doing so, he hit a pocket of turbulence that became more severe as time progressed. Jack uneasily checked his seatbelt and then held on tightly to his seat. The turbulence continued for some time longer before easing. As Jack relaxed, he became more excited of what he had seen in his dream, proving he was heading in the right direction.

About an hour later, the pilot made an announcement: "We are approaching Libya. In a short time, we will start our descent. Due to a strong head wind, we are expecting another bout of powerful turbulence ahead. Please stay calm. Our plane is able to handle this kind of turbulence. For your safety, remain seated and keep your seatbelts fastened."

As they descended, the shuddering of the plane became increasingly powerful. The plane lurched violently to the left then suddenly to the right as if the pilot had lost all control.

All the while, Jack's insides coiled and his surroundings clouded. He couldn't see, but felt death's cool hand reach out towards him. A face like the sun emerged from those dark clouds. The child was looking at him, and Jack was in great shock. Then the images dissipated and erased themselves from his mind. He excitedly whispered to himself, "But it was not a dream." *But was it possible the effect of the powerful turbulence had caused his imagination to play a trick on him?*

Another announcement that comforted everyone came from overhead: "The severity of the turbulence will disappear shortly as the moisture of the sea pushes the dust cloud away from us."

As Jack looked out of his window, he saw the large aircraft carrier anchored a short distance away. But the colour of the sea, due to the sand in the air, was stained a sinister red. It looked like the ship was sailing on a lake of blood. Once they had landed, Jack realised the enormity of the ship.

As they descended, the shuddering of the plane became increasingly powerful. The plane lurched violently to the left then suddenly to the right as if the pilot had lost all control.

The ship's commander, Admiral Longmann, greeted them on deck and invited them to a welcome dinner later that evening.

After dinner, the Admiral stood and raised his glass. "General Watson, it's a great honour and privilege for us to host you and your esteemed colleagues," he said. "I hope you rest well tonight. As you know, when you make land in Libya tomorrow morning, a long and tiring desert journey awaits you and your team."

Jack woke early the next morning, having slept very well in his luxury cabin after such a tiring journey. When he looked out of the window of his cabin, he saw that the ship had been anchored at port. There were a variety of other ships also anchored in the harbour. Some of these were civilian ships while others were Marine. As he watched from his porthole, Jack saw chrome chests being carried from one civilian ship onto a Marine ship. *How odd. What could be inside those chests?* No matter how much he wanted to know, he knew from past experience never to question military personnel. After all, he had to avoid anything that would jeopardise his own journey.

After breakfast, they left the ship in a convoy. Fifty more Marine personnel joined them, but they did not look like standard soldiers. The General had requested them, and they looked more like Special Forces. It was obvious the General prioritised the safety of the camp. The chrome chests were carried by a vehicle at the front of the convoy, which also carried more than half of the soldiers. Jack realised the chests were kept at a safe distance from the rest of the convoy.

As he watched from his porthole, Jack saw chrome chests being carried from one civilian ship onto a Marine ship. How odd. What could be inside those chests?

After a day and a half long journey, the convoy reached camp headquarters in the Sahara. Everyone was very tired, but the journey had been made more comfortable because the sandstorm had blanketed the sky, cooling the desert. Jack saw in the centre of the camp two gigantic satellite dishes that pointed west. A tall fence with layers of barbed wire encased them. While gazing out past the confines of the camp, Jack noticed that the dust storm had done away with the horizon. The sky was indistinguishable from the ground. Both had the same ominous colour.

With the help of a soldier, Jack found his tent. "Sir, the inside is much better than it looks," the soldier said. He was certainly correct; the inside was surprisingly comfortable.

After Jack exited his tent, he saw Colonel McKenzie and asked how far the closest settlement was.

The Colonel told him the closest city was 70km north, but 5km south of the camp was a small Berber village.

The existence of a village this close excited Jack. There could be witnesses who would be able to report any anomalies since the earthquake. He thought to himself, *at first chance I must get to that village.*

As Jack entered the central tent of the compound, he was overwhelmed by the technical infrastructure. In the main room, there were three gigantic screens. One was connected to NASA, another to the National Security headquarters. The third screen, between the other two, was misty and seemed to be trying to attain images of the area surrounding the energy wall. Unfortunately, the sandstorm made it impossible to see much.

"Tomorrow morning, before dawn, the team will depart," the General said, rising from his seat. "Our goal is to pass through the storm and get as close as possible to the energy wall. Under the leadership of the Colonel, ten specially equipped soldiers will also take part in the mission. After the closest safe point to the wall has been determined, we will start working."

"Sir," Jack said. The General nodded as if to give him permission to speak.

"With your permission," Jack started, "I would like to visit the small village 5km south of us today before the team leaves tomorrow. In my experience, speaking to the locals who are directly affected by an incident, such as this, can be very helpful."

"Among us, we have one soldier who can speak the local Berberic language," the General said. "You may visit the village this afternoon but take along a few other soldiers to accompany you."

Without losing any time, Jack and four soldiers hit the road. When they reached the village, they were welcomed with sincere smiles by the villagers who had been watching the camp. He learned that more than three hundred people were living in the village. Surprisingly, the majority of the villagers were older in age but still appeared healthy and exuberant.

The Chief of the village, an older man, stretched out his wooden scepter to Jack and the soldiers in a sign of friendship. Bowing slightly, "Welcome."

The place where they had gathered was right beside an ancient well the villagers thought to be divine. The Colonel had spoken of this well as the only source of water in the region.

One of the soldiers stepped forward and began to translate. The inhabitants were obviously surprised that an outsider was speaking their language.

Jack's first question pertained to why there were so many older people in the town.

The Chief, stating his own age, started to share the secret to their long lives. He pointed at the well with his wooden scepter. "This is not just an ordinary well."

He told of how there was no other water source in the area, and of how this water source had suddenly appeared miraculously many years ago.

"According to my ancestors, this well is as old as mankind. Its water is magical, and those who drink from it live extraordinarily long lives. As word spread of the properties of this water, people began to abuse it, and it became tainted. After a while, the well dried up. That was until the recent earthquake."

Jack believed the legend was another clue pointing to how close he was to the impending answer. Since waking up from that

"According to my ancestors, this well is as old as mankind. Its water is magical, and those who drink from it live extraordinarily long lives..."

dream, he felt as though his senses had sharpened. This was his life's purpose and everything else was a distraction. The clue he had spent years waiting for was finally revealed, and now it was pulling him like a magnet into the unknown. He knew it wasn't long before he would escape from the labyrinth of deception that had so cruelly imprisoned him.

The Chief continued speaking of how an ancient prophecy had been realised on the day of the earthquake. According to the legend, the waters of the dried up well would one day flow once more with ancient magical power. That day, immediately after the earthquake, an unusual light illuminated the well, and the waters of the well overflowed.

The Chief described the regenerative properties of the water; the sick became healthy and the elderly felt as strong as they had in their younger years.

"Look," he said, brandishing his scepter. "Before the earthquake, this was my faithful walking stick. But now, I don't need it. I can walk painlessly again. I can even run. I feel powerful. This well, flowing with its ancient power, has gifted us immortality. I am 117 years old! Most of my people are older than 100!"

"Before the earthquake, this was my faithful walking stick. But now, I don't need it. I can walk painlessly again. I can even run. I feel powerful. This well, flowing with its ancient power, has gifted us immortality. I am 117 years old! Most of my people are older than 100!"

Turning to the soldiers beside him, Jack said, "We need to take water samples back with us."

"Right away, Mr. Lawrence," the soldiers replied.

Turning back to the Chief, Jack asked, "Is there anything else that we should know about? Does anything seem out of place since the earthquake?"

"The air."

"What about it?"

The Chief spoke of the very dry climate in their village. Since the village was close to the desert, water has long been a scarcity. But since the earthquake, the moisture levels in the air have risen significantly. In fact, some of the crops haven't been watered for two days, but they look just as hydrated. The days have also been much cooler.

Obviously, this thing is not just in the water, but also in the air. The earthquake was a very unfamiliar event to the villagers, and it definitely scared them. But the changes that followed led them to consider the earthquake a miracle.

Like the Chief had earnestly said, the villagers truly believed the prophecy had come to pass.

Jack thanked the Chief, and the villagers warmly sent them on their way. While leaving the village, Jack turned back one more time and looked at the village gratefully. Jack was leaving with an indescribable excitement; he had found the proof he had for years searched for, and he had found it in the middle of a desert.

GUVERNIA PARADISE

CHAPTER IV — THE MIRACLE ELEMENT

JACK AND THE SOLDIERS QUICKLY LEFT THE village and raced back to the compound. The General had warned them to return before nightfall. The day had escaped them without notice, not that it mattered since Jack found the evidence he needed to prove what he'd seen had not been a dream. While looking inside one of the sample test tubes of water, his stomach churned. He tightened his grip on the tube, suddenly getting worried it would slip from his grasp. Jack thought he had seen those same colours, so he raised his head and looked towards the sky. Doing this, he realised that the colour of the sky had changed. And, strangely, the concentration of the sand in the air had settled.

Turning to the soldier beside him, he said, "Look to the sky. Do you see that?"

"The sky is clearing," the soldier said with a nod. "But our indicators tell us our visibility is still restricted."

On the way back to the compound, Jack thought of the village and the villagers. It was obvious that whatever the abnormalities were, they had mixed into the water and air since the day of the earthquake. He impatiently wanted to know the analysis results, but he was certain the water's source was somehow connected to the city among the sands.

When they reached the camp, Colonel McKenzie greeted them.

"How did your expedition go?" she asked. "Did you find anything worthwhile?"

"Definitely," Jack replied. "Directly after the earthquake, some unexpected physical changes took place in the area's water and atmospheric moisture levels. These changes are not coincidental."

"Even though most of the villagers are older than 100 years, they still look abnormally strong and healthy. The villagers connect their vitality to a so-called magical well in their village. According to local legend, the once empty well would one day overflow and regain its former power. The prophecy was realised the day of the earthquake. An overflowing well in the desert? It's a miracle. We brought back water samples to test."

"Very well done," the Colonel said. "The General doesn't want to miss anything."

Taking the water samples from Jack, the Colonel delivered them to the General's office.

"Sir, with your permission I would like to analyse some water samples brought back by Jack and his team. We believe the earthquake caused unusual atmospheric changes."

"Really?" the General eagerly said. "What type of changes?" he asked the Colonel. She quickly explained to him all that Jack had told her.

The General, taking the water samples into his hand, pondered.

Taking a deep breath, the General spoke, "We are facing a very serious situation. The water you brought back from the village contains an unidentifiable element."

"Colonel, undertake the necessary tests and immediately inform me of the results," the General ordered.

"Yes, Sir," the Colonel said and hurried out of the General's office and into the research lab.

The Colonel entered the second tent, containing the research laboratory. After a while, she returned to the General's office with an expression of shock.

Jack overheard the General loudly repeating the same question, "Are you sure? Could there be a mistake? A miscalculation?"

"No, Sir. We undertook the experiment three times to make sure our readings were correct. We obtained the same results every time."

Jack was already certain of an abnormality in the water. The villagers themselves were enough proof. As the Chief had made clear, the water had special properties. The question that remained was the location of the original water source.

The General quickly left his office. He came eye to eye with Jack, who was waiting just outside of his tent. The General's face expressed grave concern.

"What is it, General?" Jack asked.

Taking a deep breath, the General spoke, "We are facing a very serious situation. The water you brought back from the village contains an unidentifiable element."

Looking worried, he asked Jack, "Did you or any of your men drink the water?"

"No, Sir," Jack responded.

"The research officer is studying the effects of the unknown element on living organisms. He's thinking it combined with the water when the earthquake hit."

Suddenly, the research officer burst in and ran up to the General. "Sir, may I speak privately with you?"

The General was silent for a second. "You can share it here," he said. "From now on we will share our information cooperatively. This will help us with a more thorough analysis and increase our work capabilities."

"The foreign element has a different genetic makeup than any other known structures!"

"What do you mean?" the General asked.

"This thing appears to be not from our world!" The research officer continued, "When it interacts with plant matter, an incredible change occurs in its natural processes."

"What do you mean? What kind of change?" the General asked, frowning. "Is this a deformity? If so, we may be facing an immense threat."

"No, no, Sir," the research officer said. "Genetically, there is no problem. It doesn't harm the DNA structure at all. In fact, it seems to regenerate it. It may be too early to assume, but this foreign element basically recodes the organism's DNA. At the same time, it accelerates the natural processes faster than we've ever seen. When the element affects a seed, it germinates in a few seconds and grows at a supernatural rate. When it is injected into green plants, the chlorophyll levels in the plant multiply, even in the absence of sunlight. The sap inside of the plant also multiplies," he explained.

"So you're saying there are no negative side effects?"

"No, Sir—the exact opposite," the officer said. "That is what I was trying to say. This thing is supernatural—a miracle element. Whatever exists inside of it is revolutionary to genetic engineering."

"The solution to drought and starvation all over the world could be hidden inside of this new element. It might even be able to sustain life without sunlight."

When Jack heard this, he was reminded of the documentary about the starving African population the night before his dream, the expression of bewilderment betrayed his steely exterior.

"What is it, Mr. Lawrence?" the General asked. For a second, Jack felt like he had been caught in a trap. But then he thought this could be his chance.

"Mr. Lawrence, if you would like to share your thoughts, please do so for all of us to hear."

Jack stopped for a second, but he knew that, even if partly, he had to share something.

"Yes, I have something to share," he said.

Everyone turned, eyeing him curiously.

"Two days before the earthquake, I was watching a documentary on Africa, *Dark Continent's Dark Fate*. It broadcasted the atrocities of drought, starvation, genocidal dictators, and finally an image of a starving child curled up on the ground. My heart broke for this suffering child. No one should starve to death. But that night, I had a dream. The events that have transpired over the past few days here happened exactly as they had in my dream. In it, I found myself in an African desert, looking out over the endless desert sands. But then a tremendous tremor took place; it was an earthquake."

"Genetically, there is no problem. It doesn't harm the DNA structure at all. In fact, it seems to regenerate it. It may be too early to assume, but this foreign element basically recodes the organism's DNA. At the same time, it accelerates the natural processes faster than we've ever seen..."

Jack ignored the appalled expressions from his peers and continued his story.

"A large sandstorm followed, but as it settled, a city, encompassed by a rainbow light, rose from beneath the sands. I saw a golden-haired child at the front gate, sifting sand through his fingers. The child then beckoned me to the light beyond the city gates. I know all of this sounds crazy, but I'm determined to see what lies beyond the energy wall. With your permission, General, I would like to accompany the team that is leaving tomorrow morning."

"Be careful out there. You must keep a safe distance between the energy wall and you. Remember: do not approach the mysterious light."

After thinking, the General responded, "Mr. Lawrence, you may join the team..."

"Thank you, General."

"But," the General continued, "you are not to approach that wall until we know what we are dealing with. Do you understand? You will have to conduct your investigation from a distance—for your own safety. We still don't quite know what this is, and neither do we know what type of threat it might be. Dismissed."

The Colonel approached Jack, offering her reassurance. "I believe you, Mr. Lawrence. Welcome to the team."

"Thank you," Jack responded.

"As you know, we have a long road ahead of us tomorrow. So I wish you a sound and restful sleep."

"Thank you, Colonel," Jack said, nodding. "Goodnight."
Then stopping for a second, "Colonel, please call me Jack."

"Very well. Goodnight, Jack," the Colonel said.

Smiling, Jack left for his tent.

As Jack stretched out in his cot he couldn't stop thinking about the child who continued to appear to him in his dreams. His excitement prevented him from falling asleep.

***

Early the next morning, a voice woke him up. When Jack opened his eyes, he saw that the sky was still dark.

"Mr. Lawrence, in half an hour you will start your journey. The team has to get well on their way before the sun rises," the soldier said.

A treacherous journey southwards awaited them. The team consisted of the Colonel, Jack, and ten soldiers. They had all gathered at camp headquarters to outfit themselves in specially equipped camouflaged uniforms for protection against the sand and heat.

After giving a short protocol speech on the importance of the mission, the General said, "Be careful out there. You must keep a safe distance between the energy wall and you. Remember: do not approach the mysterious light."

This warning unnerved Jack. He knew for a certainty that to fully understand his dreams, he would have to defy the General's orders and enter the light.

GUVERNIA PARADISE

CHAPTER V — THE QUADRONIA GATE

THE HARSH CONDITIONS HAD HINDERED THE team's journey, and they were now two hours behind schedule. The slippery sand slowed the vehicles, even though they were designed and equipped for the desert.

The day began to dawn as the deep red in the sky gradually became a beautiful orange. The rising sun provided much needed light to aid navigation; however, the convoy of soldiers knew that with sun would come the sweltering heat. The soldier in charge of the radar broke the silence.

"There's something unnatural about the air. The sun should be well up into the sky by now, but the temperatures remain the same. In fact, the farther south we move, the lower the temperatures become."

"Are you sure?" the Colonel asked, obviously confused. "There isn't a problem with the thermometer, is there?"

"Yes, Ma'am. I'm sure," another soldier responded. "The measurements are exactly the same on mine. The temperature is almost ten degrees lower than it should be. Something is wrong."

How can this be? The Colonel wondered.

"Ma'am! Ma'am!" Another soldier called out frantically. "As of now, the temperature is 28°C!"

Turning to the soldier beside him, Jack asked, "In that case, can we take off our camouflage uniforms?"

"A thick layer of sand is still in the air, so we should continue wearing the uniforms," the soldier responded.

Another half hour passed when they realised that a shadow was stretching out from the ground ahead of them.

The driver quickly hit the brakes. The shadow looked like a gigantic snake and undulated intimidatingly. The convoy froze, trying to grasp what it was. It did not look like anything they had ever seen before. According to military research, no living creature was supposed to inhabit the area. As if it wasn't already unusual that the temperature was dropping, the presence of this unidentified creature had caused tension among the team. In the known world, a creature this large didn't exist. Whatever

"There's something unnatural about the air. The sun should be well up into the sky by now, but the temperatures remain the same. In fact, the farther south we move, the lower the temperatures become."

this thing was in front of them, it definitely did not belong to their world. Judging by its size, if it was dangerous, they were unlikely to survive.

One of the soldiers whispered, "Sir, the temperature has dropped to 25°."

Turning to the Colonel, Jack said, "To learn what this massive creature is, we have to get closer to it; we can't just sit here waiting."

Looking at the driver, the Colonel ordered, "Carefully move towards it."

Five soldiers toward the back held their weapons pointed toward the unidentified creature and squinted their eyes, watching it carefully. The driver moved inches at a time and often looked at the Colonel as if waiting for the command to halt. The accumulating beads of sweat and trembling hands made it obvious that he was nervous.

The desert surface had transformed into something similar to the Amazon rainforest. A variety of plant life covered what should have been desert.

One of the soldiers scoping out the surroundings suddenly pointed ahead. "Colonel, look! It's—they are plants, and they're everywhere!"

"What? That's impossible!" she said, taking off her sunglasses and holding her binoculars up to her eyes. "According to our coordinates, there should be nothing but sand out here..."

The plants were thriving with life. The desert surface had transformed into something similar to the Amazon rainforest. A variety of plant life covered what should have been desert.

"Are we going in the right direction?" the Colonel asked one of the soldiers.

"I'm sure there is a practical explanation for this, and sometime or another, we will find it!" Jack told the Colonel.

This abundant life found on the barren desert soil had delighted and joyed Jack. It was as if a death swamp had dried up here. He freely filled his lungs with the fresh air, doing so again and again. Even the aroma of the air seemed to hold something familiar to him. Jack, noticing how the evidence now revealed themselves without suspicion, thought he must continue on his journey. The eagerness and impatience within his heart was increasing rapidly, and Jack looked forward to reaching the door, the energy wall.

As they continued moving south, the concentration of plants started to increase. However, they hadn't encountered a single water source. While gazing at the remarkable foliage that stretched out in front of them, he recalled the words of the research officer and those of the villagers. This new element caused these plants to exist, even during the deficiency of water and sunlight. This thing was in the air and all over the place. As they approached the energy wall, the plants' tissue grew and expanded so much that the effect mirrored a forest. Jack again remembered more of the words of the research officer: "This element does not belong to our world." Jack knew where this element belonged. He knew where it was coming from. While pondering deeply on these things, he heard the Colonel speak.

The Colonel was telling the soldiers that they had approached the energy wall and would stop shortly. "How far from it?" Jack enthusiastically asked. "In half a hour, we will reach our safe point, reaching our goal and crossing the necessary border," she answered. As she said this, Jack's heart started beating faster. While everyone waited anxiously, Jack felt quite the opposite. He so desperately wanted to reach the gate. He had, after all, been waiting for years. Jack did not have the patience to wait any longer. He held an overwhelming feeling he was about to meet an old friend he had been torn away from.

As they now began to see the sky wrapped in an incomparable metallic colour, they realised they were only a short distance away from the energy wall. Sand in the air started to scatter and reveal a bright clear sky. The Colonel finally gave the driver the order to stop.

"Ma'am, look!" A soldier at the front pointed. "The wall of blue light!"

As they carefully approached their predetermined border, the sky cleared up completely. This was the eye of the storm, but an unnerving quiet had fallen over the desert. The wall of light could be seen clearly from their position. The colour of the light carried a tone of blue they had never witnessed before. The wall resembled a massive column that reached out to the sky. The whole team was frozen, staring at the column of light as if they had been bewitched. The light, in an irresistible fashion, pulled them towards it. All of the worries and fears in their minds had been replaced by a deep calmness and sense of awe. Neither Jack nor the Colonel could remember the General's warning:

Do not move past the security border toward the light!

The plants surrounding the wall had been integrated within the light. They shook as if dancing with divine magnificence. The light and everything that surrounded it were in deep harmony with one another, embracing Jack and the convoy of soldiers.

The first thing they felt in their hearts was an innocence similar to that of a baby's, untainted by the world. They started to tear up. Even though they had never experienced this feeling before, the feeling seemed altogether familiar. They felt for the first time perfect and complete in their being. This caused an indescribable happiness and relaxation. The thing in the light seemed to accept them without any expectations or conditions.

The wall of light could be seen clearly from their position. The colour of the light carried a tone of blue they had never witnessed before. The wall resembled a massive column that reached out to the sky.

Suddenly, shadows appeared from within the wall, arousing them from their sweet dream.

GUVERNIA PARADISE

CHAPTER VI — BEYOND THE WALL

JACK AND THE TEAM HELD THEIR BREATH, waiting for the shadows to emerge from the light. The distance between them and the wall was only a hundred meters, well past the safe point. But they did not care. Two animals suddenly appeared from the column of light: a lion and a gazelle. The animals looked at Jack and the team carefully as if waiting for a command. They looked back at the two animals, frozen in shock.

The gazelle approached the lion and then leaned upon its mane. In response, the lion tenderly licked it as it would a cub.

"This is impossible!" the Colonel exclaimed. Then, something remarkable happened. The lion dipped its head and ripped a cluster of grass from the ground and began to eat. The gazelle followed suit.

"Since when can a lion and its prey coexist so peace-fully? I have never seen an herbivorous lion before! What is this place? We seem to have come across an oasis. It should be sweltering here, but the temperature is a pleasant 25 degrees."

"They look nothing more like trained domestic animals," mused Jack.

"Yeah, but you can't train lions to eat plants," the Colonel said, annoyed.

"I know, but like you said, something is different about this place. Did anyone else feel a strange sense of peace as if you were complete?"

The soldiers nodded in agreement.

One soldier said, "Looking at the light, my gun suddenly felt unfamiliar, as though it didn't belong to me. It felt heavy." The other soldiers had already thrown their weapons to the ground.

"My mind is telling me you should pick up your weapons quickly," the Colonel told the soldiers. "But my heart is telling me otherwise. We don't need them anymore. We are safe. There's a correlation between what we saw at the village and what is happening now. A new age is starting in this region and possibly the whole world. This situation exceeds mankind and our understanding of nature."

The gazelle approached the lion and then leaned upon its mane. In response, the lion tenderly licked it as it would a cub.

***

Jack knew he was closer than ever to the answers he searched for. The colours he passionately longed for were all beyond this wall. He couldn't stand it any longer and wanted to run into it. He stared up at the extraordinarily bright wall, overcome with the urge to run towards it. Suddenly, he heard a whisper from beyond the wall that resonated with the desire he felt deep within.

Another shadow slowly appeared from behind the wall. This shadow looked very different from the first two and moved much more cautiously.

"Look, something's coming!" a soldier shouted.

Looking carefully at the shadow, the team realised it was the silhouette of a human. The shadow was slowly moving through the light, first revealing his head before leaping out in front of the unit of soldiers.

"...A new age is starting in this region and possibly the whole world. This situation exceeds mankind and our understanding of nature."

It was a child. Jack's heart lurched. The child from his dreams. The child with the shining golden hair. The child from the city beneath the sands.

He knelt to the ground, and Jack quickly remembered this scene from his dream. He knew what the child was going to do. The child picked up a handful of sand and scattered it into the air. The sand under the sun shone like gold dust. The child, as he watched the sand sprinkle through the air, laughed deeply. As he laughed, Jack and the soldiers were swept away by a tide of joy. Without even realising it, they all broke into laughter.

Breathlessly, Jack shouted, "I can't believe it!" The laughter had broken the chains of inhibition within Jack, and he felt an indescribable freedom.

The child looked at them and smiled.

"God!" The Colonel said, "That is the most beautiful smile I have ever seen."

The boy's smile charmed the convoy, leaving them exposed and without any memory of the General's orders.

The child looked to be a mere ten years of age. But the intensity of his gaze carried a maturity beyond his age. The child wore a robe of ivory and glittering gold and silver, which shone under the light of the desert sun. His stunning blue eyes, eyes that almost bore into the souls of those watching him, elicited a wisdom that was well beyond his years.

"Did you see his agility and that incredible leap?" The Colonel whispered to the soldier beside her.

"Colonel, I've never seen someone so fast—not even in the navy!" The soldier responded.

When the Colonel spoke, the child eyed her, seemingly listening to the conversation, despite being so far away.

Jack, unable to look away from the child, knew this was not the first time they had met.

"Ma'am, do you think he can speak our language or even understand us?" One of the soldiers asked the Colonel.

"I don't know if he can understand us or not, but he can certainly hear us," she responded.

Now looking at Jack, the child said, "I understand." The innocence in his voice and his warm, extraordinary timbre gave him an immediate sense of trust.

"What's your name?" Jack asked.

"Argen," the child replied.

"My name is Jack."

"Jack," the child repeated, sending a jolt of electricity through Jack. He had waited for years to hear the child's voice.

"What are you doing here?" Jack asked excitedly. "I mean, where do you come from?"

"Guvernia," the child responded. As he said the word, everything grew brighter in brilliance around them, and the column of light released a magnetic sound. It was obvious that everything around here was connected to Guvernia.

"Where is Guvernia?" Jack asked. The child raised his arm and then pointed at the column of light.

"I would really like to see Guvernia," Jack said. "Can I go inside?"

This seemed to surprise Argen.

"You may come inside if you wish."

The child smiled at Jack.

GUVERNIA PARADISE

CHAPTER VII — GUVERNIA

JACK HAD BEEN ON MANY JOURNEYS DURING HIS lifetime. However, the one he was about to embark on was something he had waited on for years. He fidgeted with excitement, unable to calm his nerves. He took a deep breath, gazing at the brilliantly illuminated gate in awe. He still couldn't believe he was here, standing in front of the gate he had dreamed about for so many years. The mysterious realm he had yearned to reunite with was right in front of him.

Jack looked at the foreign but so familiar child who walked ahead of him with confident steps. At the same time, Argen turned around, smiling at Jack as if to encourage him. But Jack soon stopped and turned around. He saw the Colonel and soldiers behind him, and he now felt this would be the last time he would see them. The Colonel and soldiers also looked at Jack for a long time, not saying a word. It was a quiet parting but not at all sad.

"I'll return shortly," Jack said, smiling at them. In actual fact, he had no idea when he would return if ever.

Just as the child entered the shining column of light, he turned once more to reassure Jack. Then he slowly became engulfed by it. As Jack touched the wall, he felt his heart shudder at the thought of leaving behind all he knew and all he had learned. But Jack did not shelter any doubt of whether he should do it or not. Quite the opposite, he really wanted to do it more than anything else. Jack turned and glanced back at the world he knew, one last time, before it disappeared. But as he did, he was surprised to see that everything looked different. It was now grey, colourless, and dull. It was not the world that had changed, but Jack's eyes. The Colonel and soldiers who had been left at the entrance saw the same strange light resembling the gate shining from his eyes.

As Jack moved into the column of light, he heard an extraordinary melody calling for him. It was Argen. But now his voice sounded very different. He could now hear the voice not just with his ears but also with all of his being.

When Argen saw Jack, he gave a laugh similar to the one he had given outside, and Jack responded with his own laughter.

For no reason, they looked and each other and laughed heartily for a long time.

"Argen," Jack gasped, "why does it feel like I have known you for a long time?"

Argen laughed again. "When we enter the Quadronia Gate, we are no longer bound to your mortal and limited understanding of time."

As they moved closer to Guvernia, time slowed down. The city beyond the gates was a place of serenity—a stark contrast to the desert they left behind.

"In a short time, Guvernia will emerge," Argen informed Jack.

The mortal world was disappearing behind them, and soon Jack would enter the eternal world of Guvernia, a place unfathomable to the imagination. Though the modern world had no recollection of its beauty, Guvernia's secrets had been stowed away into the furthest reaches of the heart and mind, across entire generations, only prompting its people through dreams, reminding them of a homeland where there was only life, totally rid of death.

***

Not everyone could be as fortunate as Jack Lawrence. He had cursed the unfairness of death while mourning his father. While he pondered the possibility of reversing death, Jack had the dream that began it all. He knew now that the place he had dreamed about was Guvernia. That night, Jack's subconscious created a bond between him and the mainland, using the secrets stowed away in dreams. But this was not only done by his subconscious. He had received help. Someone from Guvernia, someone from within, had created this deep bond—this powerful connection.

Just as Jack was about to enter Guvernia, he strangely remembered the words of his father, Graham:

"Remember, life is like a game of hide and seek. The answers are just waiting to be found."

In surprise, Jack saw the flashback of that morning—his father turning to wave at Jack before he left. The words of his father echoed through his mind, "I'll be back before the weekend."

I wish I could turn back time. Go back and stop my father from going on that trip.

Graham was an experienced cargo ship captain. He would sail cargo between South and North America. Jack had thought this would be like many of his countless trips. He eagerly waited for the fish hunt he and his father had planned for that weekend. It was Jack's duty to prepare the fishing rods and bait. Since his early childhood, he had gone with his father on fishing trips to rivers or lakes in the area, and both he and his father enjoyed their time together.

Jack remembered the first fish he caught with his father. He was only six-years-old and had reeled in a fat catfish. The fish had been so large that Jack had almost dropped his fishing rod.

"Daddy, help me!" Jack had screamed. His father had quickly come to his aid and helped Jack pull it in the bucket himself.

"Good job, Jack. You are a great fisherman," his father beamed. "Look at that! You have caught a chubby catfish!"

He remembered how proud his father had been. What it would mean to have him here now.

"Dad, more fish! I want to catch more fish!" he had started screaming.

"No, no, Jack," his father responded. "The purpose is not to catch more fish. If that were the case, we would buy them at the store. No, the important thing is the process."

During the following years, Jack had understood what his father had meant. The fish didn't even matter anymore. The important thing had been the time spent with his father.

Jack felt he was reliving the moment the authorities had called to inform his family of Graham's death. It was like he could hear his mother's sobs all of over again; she screamed out for her husband, refusing to believe he was dead. On the inside, Jack felt a feeling of searing yet icy emptiness growing that couldn't be stopped, no matter how hard he tried. But there remained a voice that kept nagging at Jack. A voice that told him death was unnatural and could be cured. But where had that voice come from?

Just as Jack was about to enter Guvernia, he strangely remembered the words of his father, Graham: "Remember, life is like a game of hide and seek. The answers are just waiting to be found."

According to the authorities, his ship had been caught in an unexpected storm. The last SOS call received from the vessel had informed the authorities it was about to capsize. The ship had sunk in the middle of the ocean, far from any port. The Coast Guard could not reach the ship in time, and the crew perished under the churning waves. The authorities had described the incident as though the ocean had swallowed up the vessel because the shipwreck couldn't be located. Rescuers searched the area for days, with no sign of the ship.

While Jack flicked through this old album of painful memories, Argen's powerfully bright face seemed to accompany Jack in those moments.

"Jack, we are about to enter Guvernia," Argen smiled. "At first, you won't be able to look at Solare. But don't worry, Solare will quickly fix your eyes, so it can reveal itself."

Suddenly, a bright light, brighter than anything he had ever seen before, blinded him.

With tears, he stared at the flowers and the colours painted upon the soil that so tenderly hugged the flowers. Everything here, with their dazzling magnificence, captivated the eye.

Jack surrendered to the sensation, letting the feeling of relaxation wash over him. He felt free, consumed with pure happiness. It was a feeling unlike any other. He then opened his eyes, and looked at Argen in surprise.

"Argen, you've changed!" Jack exclaimed. "You look even brighter!"

"No," Argen chuckled. "Your eyes have changed. Solare brightened and illuminated your eyes."

Jack's focus shifted from Argen as he took in his surroundings.

Bewildered, Jack said, "Look at the flowers! They are looking at me!"

As Jack took a step, the flowers politely moved sideways to make room for him.

"I recognise these colours. This is..." He paused, overcome with emotion.

Jack wanted to raise his head but couldn't. With tears, he stared at the flowers and the colours painted upon the soil that so tenderly hugged the flowers. Everything here, with their dazzling magnificence, captivated the eye. The soil made it clear that it was alive, for it kept changing its velvet colour brilliantly. Jack was unable to look away from the flowers, for they contained those magical colours he had wished so much to see. These colours anchored Jack's heart to the coast of Guvernia.

"Don't rush," Argen told Jack. "Unlike your world, in this world there is no past or future. There exists the present moment only. Enjoy it."

It was then that Jack realised he had met the architect of the past and of the future—the master of time. Throughout his entire life, Jack had ignored the power of the moment by running between the shadows of the past and the curtains of the future.

When Jack looked up, he saw the gigantic trees of the forest he was in. The trees were singing to one another. The song of the forest that steadily rose with the soft, sweet breeze of the wind was the most beautiful song Jack had ever heard.

"Solare is the inextinguishable light of Guvernia," Argen explained. "Our hearts and our thoughts are enlightened by Solare. Everything you see in Guvernia is actually a reflection of its light and love. With its immortal presence, it gifts anything it shines upon with its immortality. But all of Solare's presence is not just its visible side. For this is only a reflection of part of its immortal presence."

Argen lifted his head and looked at a tree. "Hold onto me," he told Jack. "We're going to climb it, so we can see our surroundings better from its vantage."

Jack held onto Argen's small hands. With a power and speed that shocked Jack, Argen jumped onto the lower branches of the canopy.

"How did you do that?" Jack asked. Argen didn't understand Jack's question. In Guvernia, Argen had never experienced limitations—nothing was impossible.

Argen looked at Jack and smiled, not answering his question.

Jack, as he looked away from Argen, found himself looking at a view more beautiful than anything he had ever seen. Facing this breath-taking beauty, he first laughed but began to sob like a small child. Even after losing his father, he had never before cried like this. Yet these were not tears of grief. The feelings of innocence and joy blurred together. Though tears were foreign to Guvernia, Argen knew that Jack was all right.

Under the forest, beside the sea, was a city made out of crystal. The gleaming city would make even the brightest diamonds and pearls jealous. The laughter from the Guvernians rose high above the city and could be heard all the way to where Jack stood.

"This is the most beautiful thing I've ever seen!" Jack exclaimed.

"That is where our hearts lie—our home, Eterno," Argen said devotedly.

This was the city of the immortals. The city's spirit fed off Solare's brilliance and shared the same heartbeat as its citizens.

Right beside the city, the crystal-clear ocean shone like sapphire. When Jack noticed lights glinting underneath the sun, he pointed, asking, "What are they?"

"Children collecting pearls," Argen responded. As Jack squinted his eyes and looked carefully, he saw the groups of children along the beach, laughing as they collected their treasure.

"Look at that!" The children, as they ran, were able to skim across the water. As they jumped, they rose effortlessly into the air.

"Solare is the inextinguishable light of Guvernia," Argen explained. "Our hearts and our thoughts are enlightened by Solare..."

When they dived into the water, they were as sharp as an arrow and as soft and elegant as a swan.

Jack paused, brow furrowing, "Argen, is there any danger here?"

From Argen's expression, Jack realised that Argen hadn't understood his question. Jack had to somehow explain the concept of danger.

"Look at the children," Jack started to explain. "They are jumping from great heights and can accidentally fall and get injured. What I mean—can something bad happen to them? Is there anything that could harm anyone here?"

Argen still didn't understand.

My innocent friend, you don't know how lucky you are. Jack had to somehow teach him about these things.

Jack remembered the scar he had on his arm. "Look," he said. "Do you see this? When I was a child, I fell from a tree in my garden. I broke my arm, and I had to keep it in a sling for a long time. I can remember the pain quite clearly."

The children, as they ran, were able to skim across the water. As they jumped, they rose effortlessly into the air.

Stretching out his arm, he showed Argen the old scar.

Argen reached out and slowly traced the pale raised line on Jack's skin.

He was definitely surprised. "How does this happen?" Argen asked.

"Here in Guvernia, we have been gifted with endless knowledge about our world, but we know nothing about the suffering of your world."

"So you've never been injured before? Do you even age?" Jack wondered out loud.

"What do you mean?"

"Where are your parents? Where are your grandparents?"

"All here," Argen responded.

"All?" Jack asked with surprise.

"All. In fact, their countless parents are also here. Their bodies are strong like mine and have never been injured," Argen explained.

"Doesn't anyone die here?" Jack exploded with anticipation.

Argen was totally oblivious to the concept of death.

"When someone dies, you can't ever see them again. They are gone forever," Jack said. Taking a deep breath, "It's a painful time."

Argen looked into Jack's eyes. In great surprise, he understood the concept of death.

"I lost someone whom I really loved," Jack said. Argen touched Jack and then put his hand on Jack's forehead. His eyes suddenly started to shine.

"Jack, I can see him. He isn't lost," Argen said. "He is in the middle of an ocean, living alone in a small island."

"Are you sure?"

He's not lost. I see him on the island. He thinks of you often. He wants to see you."

"Can you help me find him?" Jack pleaded.

Argen nodded with a smile. Jack was overcome with joy, letting out a small laugh in disbelief.

"Look," Argen said. "Whales are coming."

Jack looked to the water and saw the whales quickly approaching the shore, the Guvernians controlling them as if they were a ship.

"How do you control them?" Jack again wondered out loud.

"We didn't do anything," Argen explained. "It's in their nature."

Jack suddenly remembered the lion and the gazelle he had seen at the gate. The lion had been not only domesticated, but it had been an herbivore.

Do animals prey on one another here in Guvernia? Do they eat one another?" Jack asked. Once again, Argen looked at Jack in confusion.

"The world I come from is a scary place, my friend," Jack commented. "I wouldn't even begin to mention the conflicts between humans that end in death and destruction."

Trying to change the subject, Jack turned to look at the appetising fruit from the branches of the tree.

"Can you please share your fruit?" Argen asked the tree, after noticing Jack looking.

While Jack stood frozen in shock, Argen ripped off two ripe fruits from the tree. Jack watched in disbelief as new fruit instantly grew back in the place where Argen had taken from.

"How?" Jack gaped. He remembered how everything was possible in this world, and that everything existed in the moment. He was starting to comprehend the power of the moment more deeply now.

Then Jack heard the rip-roaring sound of the pearl collecting children. "They're coming! They're coming!" the children screamed.

The children boarded dolphins, which they called the "Golden Fins". After doing this, they rushed towards the incoming whales to greet the returning families. Then they jumped from the dolphins and flew toward the whales. Amidst laughter, they hugged their families, landing on the whales. The children placed the pearls they had collected from the oysters around the necks of their mothers and fathers. Their parents, in return, ripped tufts of "oceanic daffodils", a seaweed native to Guvernian waters. The oceanic daffodils were known to provoke over-whelming joy when eaten.

"Look, Jack!" Argen said excitedly. "Oceanic Daffodils. I'm sure you'll love them. You really have to try them. Come on! Let's go to Eterno."

"The world I come from is a scary place, my friend," Jack commented. "I wouldn't even begin to mention the conflicts between humans that end in death and destruction."

GUVERNIA PARADISE

CHAPTER VIII — STORM

ONE HOT AND HUMID MORNING, CAPTAIN Graham Lawrence's cargo ship left Panama en route to New York. Earlier that morning, the Captain had met with his assistant, Captain Scot, to discuss the logistics of adding six extra containers to their load. Captain Scot believed it would not cause any trouble, despite the last minute rush to get them on board. Not one to be disorganised, Captain Lawrence was hesitant about the additional cargo, especially because he didn't know what they contained. Captain Lawrence had received a call from his boss informing him that the containers must be loaded. The Captain entered his room and sat down. He glanced over at the blue picture frame on his desk—inside, a photograph of his young son Jack and wife, Caroline. The smiling faces looked back at him, filling him with a sense of reassurance and calm. "Jack, I promise that when I get back, I'm going to take you fishing," he said to himself, smiling. Graham enjoyed going fishing with his son. It had now become a family tradition of sorts.

After a long day loading the cargo ship with the extra containers, the crew was ready for bed. Captain Lawrence had lost track of time thinking of his family but climbed into bed, expecting a well-deserved sleep. There was something about being at sea that allowed him to sleep more soundly. He fell asleep as soon as his head hit the pillow.

He glanced over at the blue picture frame on his desk—inside, a photograph of his young son Jack and wife, Caroline. The smiling faces looked back at him, filling him with a sense of reassurance and calm.

The Captain heard someone knocking on his door at sunrise. Unless it was an emergency, the crew knew not to disturb him while in his quarters. The voice at the door was Captain Scot's, and he sounded very concerned.

"Captain, Captain! Wake up! It's an emergency!"

Captain Lawrence quickly dressed and opened the door.

"What's wrong, Scot?" he asked.

"Captain, a large storm is up ahead!"

"Look at the coordinates then make the necessary changes in our route, so we can bypass it. What direction is the storm coming from and how far away is it?" Captain Lawrence asked.

"Sir, the storm is approaching eastwards, but I'm afraid it's unpredictable," Captain Scot replied. "We expect to encounter it in about two and a half hours."

Studying the coordinates, Captain Lawrence was quiet for a few seconds.

"Scot, increase our speed and move us westward. We're going to try and maneuver our way around it."

Captain Scot quickly followed orders. The speed of the ship was now charging it through the waters in a westerly direction. The remaining twenty crew members, who were sleeping, suddenly woke up as the ship shook with the increased speed.

As speed dials reached code red, heavy sounds started to rise from the body of the ship. The tremors of the ship increased at an alarming rate.

The two Captains continued watching the progression of the storm from their radar screens.

Taking a deep and discouraging breath, Captain Lawrence said, "This isn't good. This storm is strong, fast, and growing more unpredictable."

"Captain! Look at the size of those waves," Scot pointed out.

"It's coming towards us with great speed. I'm afraid we are going to run into it."

"Captain, do you think our ship can handle it?"

"We have faced many storms at sea, but even I will admit this looks a little different from the other storms we have faced." Scratching his head thoughtfully, he continued, "Though risky, we need the motors running at full power. We don't have any other choice."

"Did you say full power?" Scot was surprised by the Captain's suggestion. "Captain, our motors have been on full speed since we started this journey. As you well know, it's not advised that loaded cargo ships run on full power in case of overheating. We may end up stranded in the middle of this ocean!"

"Scot, we don't have any time to waste," the Captain decided. "This is a code red emergency. The only way to bypass this storm is to run our motors on full power."

"Yes, Sir," responded his unconfident co-captain.

Slowly, Scot pushed the lever higher and higher.

Through uneasy movements, he slowly increased power to full speed. As speed dials reached code red, heavy sounds started to rise from the body of the ship. The tremors of the ship increased at an alarming rate.

"Gather everyone together," the Captain ordered Scot.

Over the intercom, Scot called for an emergency meeting. The crew gathered nervously around Captain Lawrence, waiting for him to speak.

"Gentlemen," Captain Lawrence began, "I know you are all good sailors, and we have encountered many dangers together. As you may know, we are about to face a large storm front that we cannot avoid. Our calculations predict it will develop into a hurricane once it hits the east coast, and we are doing our best to steam ahead and outrun it. This is a very fast-moving storm, so we must take measures to prepare for the worst. I predict we have about an hour until we come across the most critical point of it, so I want you all to bunker down in the lower cabins and wait for the storm to pass."

The crew left the deck immediately, obviously very concerned by what the Captain had just shared with them. Captain Lawrence and Captain Scot were left to the silence of their own thoughts.

"Captain, I can see the size of these waves on the screen. What hope do we have?"

"Scot, there is always hope. Go and join the crew down below. I'll be there shortly."

But Captain Lawrence planned on staying in the control room. He believed there was still hope, and decided he would direct the ship out of trouble. Scot looked at the Captain, knowing he couldn't change his mind. He quietly left the room.

The Captain once more thought of the photograph of his wife and son. "I yearn to see you two again," he whispered.

Though the waves around the ship were rolling slowly, the vicious ocean ahead would soon swallow them whole. The ship was thrown into darkness like the zenith of night.

He recalled the day he had taken that photograph. It had been a wonderful spring day with a cool breeze. Graham felt he could still hear the laughter of his wife and son—oh, the beautiful laughter of that day. *This must be Heaven,* the Captain thought to himself.

But his present reality was more of a nightmare. He only wished he could wake up and return to that wonderful moment of heaven he had shared with his family.

From outside the control room's window, dark clouds slowly started to materialise, encroaching maliciously on his thoughts. Everything was eerily quiet—the calm before the storm. Though the waves around the ship were rolling slowly, the vicious ocean ahead would soon swallow them whole. The ship was thrown into darkness like the zenith of night. Though it was only eight in the morning, the day became engulfed by a pitch dark. *This is probably going to be my last day alive,* the Captain suddenly thought. A scary buzzing sound started to rise, destroying the sombre silence. Captain Lawrence squinted his eyes, then looked into the storm as if he were challenging it. The storm had killed the motors, and it was pulling the ship toward it like a spider pulling at a fly trapped in its web. He desperately tried to get the engine to start, with no avail. The waves shook the cargo ship violently as if it were a small, weightless toy.

GUVERNIA PARADISE

CHAPTER IX — ETERNO

ARGEN WHISTLED WITH THE WONDROUS TIMBRE of a harp. A neigh response came from within the depths of the forest. Two ivory horses raced towards Jack and Argen.

"Look at them! Are they flying?" Jack asked with surprise, watching the horses gallop towards them effortlessly.

Argen hugged one of the horses tenderly, whispering into its ear. The horse immediately knelt before Jack, waiting for him to mount it.

"Get on its back and hold onto its mane," Argen said, smiling. "Then it will take you wherever you would like to go."

Jack politely mounted the horse. Argen climbed onto the other horse. Moving like an arrow released from its bow, they quickly raced toward Eterno.

As they approached the magnificent city, Jack remembered the words of Argen:

That is where our hearts lie—our home, Eterno.

The passion Argen felt for Eterno had awakened in Jack a deep longing for a city he had never been to. He felt this city was his home. The remarkable grandeur of the city seemed to grow as he drew closer to it. The crystals blinked, illuminating the city with a rainbow light, dancing even on the Aquarella Sea, which lay right beside the city. However, it was Jack's ignorance that blinded him from the magnificence of Solare who had caused this spectacle of beauty.

The remarkable grandeur of the city seemed to grow as he drew closer to it. The crystals blinked, illuminating the city with a rainbow light, dancing even on the Aquarella Sea.

They had finally reached the opulent streets of Eterno. They glowed with the hues of a sunset. Guvernians peacefully moved about the streets of the city.

"Gold!" Shouted Jack as he looked at the street made of shiny stones.

Jack dismounted his horse and looked around in awe as a beautiful melody filled the air.

"Can you hear that?" he whispered, so as to not interrupt the music.

Argen nodded. "That is Eterno's song. It sounds different to everyone. It seems to speak directly to whomever is listening."

Argen and the other Guvernians turned their heads toward Solare and started absorbing the melody with gripping joy.

A group of locals approached Jack and studied him carefully. But their stares were not searing as they would have been in his world. Their stares were innocent and sincere—welcoming. Somehow Jack knew that he was really back at home. This was the homeland he had passionately for years searched for, and Jack had finally reunited with his home.

Jack slowly started to comprehend that everyone who lived in Guvernia had a perfect level of consciousness. In light of this, Jack began to question many things about his own world.

"Do they know I am an outsider?" Jack whispered into Argen's ear.

"No, Jack," Argen smiled. "Under Solare's light, everyone sees everyone, and everyone knows everyone. There are no outsiders here."

As Jack heard this, he suddenly thought of the humans from his own world, and how they were strangers and enemies to one another.

In Guvernia, everyone was equal. Some things Jack found difficult to comprehend about this world. One of these was the wonderful unity that existed between the Guvernians. But what had surprised him more was there was no leader to enforce this order and unity. Jack slowly started to comprehend that everyone who lived in Guvernia had a perfect level of consciousness. In light of this, Jack began to question many things about his own world.

War was one of those things he deeply believed needed a solution. He yearned for lasting peace. Humanity had inflicted its greatest damage on itself because of wars. As he again pondered the hair triggers of war, he realised the problem was far more individualistic than shared. Like the outwardly expanding rings from skipping a stone on water, the triggers began with an individual, which rippled toward his peers and then out into the greater community, often causing divide.

The concept of diversity in Guvernia was very different. Diversity here did not alienate; it unified. Because all were equal to one another, underneath Solare, everyone knew they were special and unique. Comparison was a weed among the people, replaced with a shared admiration for those who tried to be themselves only.

Jack then realised another problem of his own world. Everyone he knew begged to be somebody else. They would spend a lifetime trying to be similar and wound up themselves, and others, in the process. They surrendered their unique natures just so they weren't ostracised from the people they desperately wanted to be a part of—the root of most world wars.

Militaries spent millions of dollars to fund an expansion of similarity and to annihilate anyone and anything different to the comfortably familiar. Jack knew humanity had to do something to stop the spreading of this life-threatening virus and, thankfully, he had just found the antidote.

Jack's thoughts played out in front of the Guvernians like a movie.

A Guvernian named Ordion approached Jack. "Your world and Guvernia are parallel worlds, but our co-existence can only be accessed when someone is dreaming. An area deep inside the Aquarella Ocean is where dreams slip through the Quadronia Gate and enter Guvernia. Argen saw yours and was able to reach you. Even if you can't remember, that's how you first met Argen. This was not a physical meeting but one of consciousness. A physical gate named Quadronia divided and connected our two worlds, but it was closed a long time before.

A few days ago, an unexpected explosion opened the Quadronia Gate, bridging our two worlds together. Since that day, the Guvernian climate has spread into your world and has begun the transformation we have been waiting for.

GUVERNIA PARADISE

CHAPTER X — TRANSFORMATION

COLONEL MCKENZIE AND THE SQUAD OF soldiers watched in surprise as Jack's silhouette disappeared into the shining blue light. They waited impatiently for his return, desperately wanting to know what lay beyond the wall of light.

"Ma'am, look!" One of the soldiers said. "Something else is approaching the gate."

Like the lion and the gazelle, the animals that exited the gate looked different from this world. Animals streamed out of the gate in a line that stretched so far that the convoy could not see each animal. The animals moved quickly and obediently as if being guided by a shepherd. They all disappeared behind a cluster of trees. As Colonel McKenzie watched in shock, she noticed the swirling sand had settled, and she could now see the true magnitude of the wall, surrounded by a lush rainforest.

Putting a hand on her forehead, she gasped, "Oh, my God! There's a forest in the middle of the Sahara!"

"Colonel, look!" a soldier pointed at a herd of gleaming white horses as they galloped towards them. "They run so fast!"

The animals had been instructed by their Guvernian masters to convert the regional creatures into their likeness. Starting in Africa, they were to spread into all the continents and be the catalysts for the long awaited transformation. A pride of lions travelled north into the territory of African lions. At first, the regional pride roared in defence of their territory and then tried to intimidate the Guvernian lions away from the area. They, however, did not succeed. Realising their efforts were not working, they started to back away from the foreigners. The Guvernian pride advanced and began to light up the area with a metallic light that shone from their eyes, stunning the regional lions. The light carried the rays of Solare, and in his presence, the entire pride of African lions became as gentle as the Guvernian lions. The Colonel and her soldiers watched from afar as this transformation took place. They couldn't believe how docile the regional lions had become after such a fierce attempt at defending their territory.

A Guvernian leopard came across a wild leopard that had just caught its prey. The leopard had a young gazelle in its mouth and was about to break its neck. It turned to look at the Guvernian leopard and suddenly a flash of light caused the gazelle to drop from the leopard's grip and onto the sand. The wild leopard began to lick the injured animal, and soon the Guvernian leopard joined it and did the same. Miraculously, the gazelle began to heal. As the gazelle stood up, it looked surprised at the leopards, and it then raced away as if nothing had happened.

The Guvernian animals were not just transforming this world' creatures, but they were also healing the wounded and disabled ones. They were bringing restoration.

As the transformation became more widespread, villagers from surrounding areas began to notice a change in the climate and the behaviour of the animals in the area. They soon informed the authorities who fast tracked the information to General Watson at the National Security army base.

***

News of the transformation had spread like wildfire around the world. Everyone was talking about the earthquake in Africa and the climate changes it had brought with it. National Security attempted unsuccessfully to put the public at ease, telling news outlets that previous reports had been exaggerated. The blue light of the Quadronia Wall did not go unnoticed, and many thrill-seekers ventured into the desert in an attempt to see it with their own eyes.

The World Peace Council scrambled to form a World Security Committee to organise military action against any possible threats to humanity. A secret meeting amongst committee members in Geneva decided to secure the desert area, to stop any members of the public going to see the wall.

The media continued to explode with theories no one was able to verify. Some thought these changes were fulfilled prophecies; some thought they were a miracle of nature; and others even proclaimed the arrival of extra-terrestrial life. The only certain thing was the growing confusion that sprung from the situation.

Jack's boss, Arnold, wanted his newspaper to be the first to report the breaking news. He hoped it would help put *Daily View* on the map. But much to his concern, he hadn't heard from Jack, who was right in the centre of the events.

***

Back at the camp, the General had arranged an emergency meeting with seasoned military personnel from around the world. Nearly fifty officials crammed into the meeting hall and waited patiently for the General to speak.

"I want to firstly welcome Professor Albert Smith, a renowned scientist who has contributed incredible DNA knowledge to the world, has honoured us here today by joining us. He has mentored many scientists all over the world, one of who is also with us today," the General announced.

There was a round of applause for Professor Smith.

The General continued, "We have recently acquired animal data of natural predators that now exhibit herbivorous tendencies. We have, therefore, invited Professor Smith along today to provide insight into this new data."

"Thank you, General." Professor Smith said as he stood.

"My colleagues and I examined and studied the well water samples you sent me, and we discovered a foreign element suspended in the water from the well. This element has a different structure to any we've seen before. A variation in DNA structure appears to be mutated. In fact, most of the structure of this element is unreadable and corrupted. Because of this, we are working to scrutinize the model of this structure, so we can read the DNA to uncover its true potential. We have no idea what it can do to the human body."

We discovered a foreign element suspended in the water from the well. This element has a different structure to any we've seen before.

"Professor, can you say with certainty this element does not belong to our world?" the General asked.

"Yes, and no," the Professor replied. "I know my answer is ambiguous, so let me explain. I believe this element may have existed in our world without us realising it. Part of the element's readable DNA sampling shows evidence that it may have been present in the human body at some stage of its development. We haven't been able to prove it yet, but I strongly believe this is the case. We have been able to discover that the element can recode plant DNA. We call this DNA restoration, and the process was a theory deemed impossible until now. This information is revolutionary for genetic engineering. The element changes the natural life cycle of its host . It basically removes the cycle. Let me explain it like this: instead of waiting a season for a plant to bear its fruit, DNA restoration takes place at such a rapid rate that the plant produces fruit instantly, without any waiting. We have named it, the 'Miracle Element.'"

The element changes the natural life cycle of its host . It basically removes the cycle. Let me explain it like this: instead of waiting a season for a plant to bear its fruit, DNA restoration takes place at such a rapid rate that the plant produces fruit instantly, without any waiting.

"Professor, could you please talk about the animals?" the General asked.

"After bringing in various predatory animals for tests, we collected DNA samples. But I would like to start by talking about the animals' temperament. These animals appear to have been completely domesticated to the point of docility. I personally think these animals have suffered a deformation," the Professor explained.

Again interrupting the Professor, the General inquired, "A deformation? Could this also happen in humans?"

"Yes," the Professor said frankly. "It's very early yet to clearly hypothesise on the effects it has on humans, but it looks as if the element has disrupted the animals' predatory instincts. It's like the gene linked to the instinct of self-protection has also been negated."

A worrying thought suddenly went through the General's mind, making him very uneasy. "What if the same thing happens to us? Will we then be incapable of protecting ourselves during a fight?"

The Professor continued to speak:

"Basically, these animals are currently not perceiving any of their surroundings as a threat. It seems as if the natural fight or flight response signals are not being sent to the brain.

"However, two lions tested here have a DNA variation that has surprised us. That DNA structure is also completely foreign to us. We have reached the conclusion it came from wherever the element in the well water originated.

"Their cells do not degenerate. They do not age and, therefore, do not die. When a cell is damaged, it immediately repairs itself. We have repeated tests multiple times. Though the results contradict all known scientific data, the results are always the same. In layman's terms, these animals with foreign DNA have immortal cells. To be sure, we shot the animals multiple times. But the animals demonstrated they can't feel pain. None of the bullets did any permanent damage.

"One other thing affected me even more deeply. The animals looked at us as if to say *'Why are you doing this to us?'*

"With ongoing testing, we may be able to use this information to eradicate our own sicknesses and diseases. We may even stop death."

A contemplative quiet fell upon the room.

GUVERNIA PARADISE

CHAPTER XI – FREEDOM

LOOKING INTO JACK'S EYES MERCIFULLY, ORION said, "I'm very sorry. I can see the world from which you came through your mind. It is full of pain and disaster. I can see the many viruses that threaten your world, even the ones that hide themselves from your kind."

Holding Jack's hand in comfort, Argen said, "Solare has given you the gift to see inside yourself. Have a look, Jack." Argen whispered.

Jack closed his eyes, venturing into his inner being. "No! No, it can't be!" he gasped in horror at what he saw. "It's me. I am the monster!"

"That's not you. You just think it is," replied Argen.

As Jack looked again, he saw that the monster was something that lived inside every human—an envious, egotistical being. It was thought to simply be part of human nature, but it wasn't.

Genetically, ego was the virus that had infected all people. Humanity's most dangerous enemy lived on the inside. It was a niggling feeling in the back of the mind, perceiving everyone else as a threat and fuelling paranoia. It caused wars, death and the destruction of humanity.

"The thing that is destroying all of you and your world is the ego that resides quietly inside you. You think this is part of your nature," Ordion said. "This enemy hates all of you and seeks to destroy you and your world, but it fools you into thinking it's helping you survive. If humankind doesn't do everything it can to eliminate ego, it will be successful in turning your world into a hellish reality.

As Jack looked again, he saw that the monster was something that lived inside every human—an envious, egotistical being. It was thought to simply be part of human nature, but it wasn't.

"In our world, no human rules over another human. We are born free and always stay free. The thing that keeps us together is not our selfish desire but our love for one another—a love tested by the freedom to love.

"When I look at your world, I see everyone has been enslaved. Everyone is ruled by a dark order. When I look at your master, I see him continually shouting 'I, me, mine.' If humankind continues to be enslaved this way, the end is in sight.

"Free will is our greatest treasure. For this reason, Jack Lawrence, you have not been completely transformed, yet.

Though you have tasted Solare's light and Guvernia's life, you are still a human ruled by your ego. The impending question we now ask you does not just weigh upon your shoulders, but because you stand here as a representative of all humankind, your answer will count for everyone. Jack Lawrence, would you like to be transformed and freed?" Ordion asked.

Doubt flashed across Jack's mind for a brief moment. "When I am transformed, will I be similar to a Guvernian? Will the monster residing in me be gone, once and for all?"

"Yes, Jack. The monster will be destroyed and its venom drawn from your veins. But whether or not you look like us will be determined by Solare," Argen replied. "After all, Solare is the source of your transformation."

Jack looked at them nervously, still a little hesitant about his decision. "I would like to proceed with the transformation."

Argen's gaze met Jack's, and for a split second, Solare's light flickered in his eyes. Jack could hear screams coming from within him. Then, like a scolded dog, the monster fled.

When Jack opened his eyes, he could see Solare as if for the first time. In shock and admiration, he looked into it. Solare started to speak to Jack through Eterno's immortal song. The melody spoke of the world that Jack's ancestors had once freely roamed. Then the song filled all of Jack's being.

Jack knew his transformation was complete. There was not a language nor word with which Jack could explain the feeling of freedom and relaxation that had come upon him. He no longer felt threatened. He did not feel fear or feel the need to defend himself. He was now the first free human living on Earth. But this wasn't the fake, selfish freedom defined by the ego; this was true freedom. Jack Lawrence could finally live without fear and love wholeheartedly.

GUVERNIA PARADISE

CHAPTER XII — RESTORATION

"GET THE SATELLITE IMAGES ON SCREEN," THE General ordered. The sky had cleared quicker than they had expected, and the satellite was now relaying clear images of the gate.

Everyone at base camp headquarters quickly assembled in the meeting hall, waiting in excitement, their eyes fixated on the screen in curiosity. No one knew what to expect. The satellite first zoomed in on the massive forest in the Sahara and then panned to the area with the blue column of light. The images slowly came into focus, and they could see the Colonel and her team in the small camp they had set up right beside the column of light.

Suddenly, there was movement from inside the Quadronia gate. The blue light intensified. The Colonel and her team, along with everyone back at headquarters, stared in shock.

When the General saw that Colonel McKenzie and her soldiers had dropped their weapons, he was enraged. "Have they lost their minds? They have breached the safety zone!" he bellowed.

"Immediately, set up an audio connection between us and Colonel McKenzie!" he ordered.

While a communication line was being established, the gate began to emit a strange metallic noise. Suddenly, the silhouette of a large crowd appeared. The General, and those around him, held their breaths, looking at the gate with popped-out eyes.

The first person to exit the gate was Jack, with an extraordinary smile on his face. The General first noticed his beaming smile and then the light that shone from his eyes. A flash of light, seemingly coming from the small child beside Jack, dropped the convoy to the ground. Colonel McKenzie and her team lay silently and motionless as if dead. Panic ran throughout base camp, the General watching helplessly as his team lay lifeless on the sand. Those at the base watched on, helplessly. Then the convoy slowly stirred back to consciousness and climbed to their feet as if nothing had happened. They looked around, eyes now shining like Jack's. They greeted the Governing's like old friends. The General felt he had lost all control.

People were still pouring out from the gate—their number too large to count. A herd of white horses then exited the gate and waited obediently for the Guvernians to mount them. The group then dispersed, heading off in all directions.

A feeling of sheer panic fell upon everyone in the meeting room.

Who were these strangers? This must definitely be some sort of an invasion.

The way their faces glowed, the light that came from their eyes, and their opulent gold and silver clothing were all foreign.

Moreover, they appeared equipped with a weapon that could enslave the global population—a weapon that had the power to control minds. If the Colonel and her team couldn't withstand it, what chance did anyone else have?

The General left the meeting room without a word of indication for his private tent. He wasted no time reaching for a secured line and dialled the office of his superior. The crisis had elevated beyond his control.

"Sir, we are facing a bigger threat than we had anticipated," the General said. "They appear human, but it's obvious they aren't from our world. It seems they have used a type of beam to take control of our soldiers' minds. In the blink of an eye, they have neutralised our dispatch team." He paused for a moment to receive his instruction.

"But, Sir, the Colonel and her team are not in our control anymore. We can't do this."

What the General was hearing did not offer him any comfort. The stress funnelled through his body, causing him to stiffen. He noticed he was clenching his fist so tightly that it had turned an empty shade of white.

"Yes, Sir," he responded. "We will leave with another team immediately."

The General ended the call and stood up. Taking a deep breath, he shouted to the guard posted outside his tent. "Soldier, get Colonel Williams over here!" he demanded.

"Yes, Sir," the soldier replied, leaving his post with haste.

There was a knock at the door. "Sir, you wanted to see me?"

"Come in. As we all just saw, we are facing imminent danger. Knowing initially this would be a dangerous mission, we equipped Colonel McKenzie and her team with the best weapons before sending them into the desert. Unfortunately, due to reasons we don't quite understand, we have completely lost our command over them. As a result, the nuclear warhead that we sent with them is ineffective. Our enemy carries a weapon that we have not yet identified. It appears to be biological in nature, almost like a laser emanating from their eyes. Though it appears harmless, it had rendered our soldiers and their weapons useless. We have to find a way to protect ourselves."

"How so, Sir?"

"First, we have to build a type of shield these weapons cannot penetrate," the General explained. "I need you to select a team to join the others. We have some scientists who have experience with this type of defence equipment. Before getting in contact with main headquarters at home, first work with our personnel here."

The General didn't support the decision made by his superiors at main headquarters, but he had no choice but to follow orders.

The General and Colonel Williams made their way to the meeting hall to address the rest of the team about their decision. The room was still alive with chatter, eyes still fixated on the screen. As the two men entered, an uneasy silence fell upon the room.

"As you have seen, our world is under threat," the General began. "We don't have any time to lose. We have to prepare ourselves against any attacks that our enemy will undertake. Let me be clear. We find ourselves at war. We will do whatever it takes to protect humanity and our planet. The first team, lead by Colonel Mackenzie, took with them a powerful explosive. But as you have seen via satellite images, the enemy has disabled our team and our initial defence strategy. We need to

They appeared equipped with a weapon that could enslave the global population—a weapon that had the power to control minds.

develop another line of defence to protect ourselves from their weapons, and fast, before we can think about sending a second team. Our enemy has already started to spread across the planet. A type of shield their light can't bypass is needed. But let me make this clear also: time is working against us. Our enemy has already, with great haste, started to move to the four corners of the planet."

The Professor raised his hand to speak.

"Yes, Professor?" the General acknowledged.

"General, we know that Jack Lawrence and the entire team are still alive. These people might not be as dangerous as we think."

"The enemy may not have harmed our team physically, but at this moment the team is under their control. Subduing our soldiers and mentally controlling them is a show of hostility. We must fight them," said the General.

Taking a deep breath, the Professor continued, "I personally do not believe this foreign civilisation is a danger to our world. Many problems in our world, I believe, can be solved if we learn from what they know. Who knows? This may be the best thing that happened to humanity. This could be a miracle."

"...the nuclear warhead that we sent with them is ineffective. Our enemy carries a weapon that we have not yet identified. It appears to be biological in nature, almost like a laser emanating from their eyes..."

"Professor, you don't understand," the General interrupted. "We don't live in a fantasy world. An enemy is out there—an enemy whose powers far exceed what we understand and who is advancing towards us. My mission is to do everything to protect the world from any possible threat. We don't just build our strategy on visible threats but also on the possibility of unseen threats. Just because our enemy is keeping our team alive, it doesn't mean they are peaceful. We must not waste any more time debating whether this is a threat or not and start formulating a plan of attack. We are doing this for humanity. Do you understand?"

The General ran a hand over his mouth, sighing. "Excuse me, Professor, don't take my speech too personally. As you can understand, this is a stressful situation. It is my priority to ensure the safety of all civilians."

The Professor shook his head in disagreement. The General did not like this silent protest made by the Professor. He shot him a harsh glare. The quiet challenge between them ended when a soldier finally spoke.

"Sir, the army has developed a shield to protect us from the enemy's laser beams and any other type of powerful lights. But without testing it, it's hard to tell whether the shield will actually work."

"That is a risk we will have to take. Colonel Williams, get your team ready and leave as soon as you can," concluded the General.

GUVERNIA PARADISE
CHAPTER XIII — KULAM BATAR

THE GUVERNIANS HAD BEGUN TO SPREAD ACROSS the globe. Their horses sprinted with ease across the world landscape as if flying. For their masters, time was of the essence.

Jack, Argen and a few other Guvernians were heading east. When Argen looked ahead with his sharp vision, he realised they were approaching the village of Kulam Batar.

Jack was feeling an indescribable excitement. This was the moment he had waited for all his life, and he knew he had been born for this purpose. His dying world had finally found the remedy it had been hoping for.

As the village came into view over the horizon, it became obvious that this village had been ravaged by drought and poverty. This was about to change.

The villagers first heard the hooves of the horses—the sound shaking the earth. The horses were foreign to the villagers, but the curious children were the first to come running out of the village. Then the remaining villagers came to greet their unexpected visitors.

Can these be the angels who have come to save us, as foretold in the old African legends? they pondered.

One of the Guvernians whistled a melody similar to that of Eterno's. As the villagers heard the magnetic sound, they gathered around the Guvernians, desperate to hear more. The melody began to make a magnetic space, and anyone who heard the sound was pulled to it without any resistance.

As the villagers settled in the melody of the Guvernians, Solare's light shone from the visitor's eyes, and Eterno's song was shared. The entire village was illuminated by Solare's light, and now this village had been freed from sickness and pain. Because Solare's lasting light had leaked into their bodies, the villagers were free from fear. No case of malaria, no case of starvation could torment them again. Not only had their bodies healed but also their minds. The once insignificant village had now reached the highest form of civilisation and culture found in all of the world.

Can these be the angels who have come to save us, as foretold in the old African legends? they pondered.

Argen knelt to the ground and then taking a handful of soil, he scattered it into the air. Jack now knew what Argen was doing. Guvernia's untainted seeds of life were meeting with the soil from the village, and the seeds of life blessed the soil eternally. From now on, poverty would be no more in this area.

With this, the dying world received new life from Guvernia's hands, and a new immortal world was rising from among the ashes.

As the Guvernians left the area, the villagers were overwhelmed with gratitude. They saw the Guvernians off in peace, waving until they were out of sight. All of their eyes and faces shone with Solare's brilliance.

Argen knelt to the ground and then taking a handful of soil, he scattered it into the air. Jack now knew what Argen was doing. Guvernia's untainted seeds of life were meeting with the soil from the village.

When Jack turned back to look at the village, his eyes met those of the town's old chief. From now on, the village would have no chief nor any soldiers. It did not need to be ruled or protected anymore.

Jack chuckled. Argen responded to Jack's laugh by giving one of his own. It was time for them to leave and spread Guvernia's gifts throughout the rest of the world.

GUVERNIA PARADISE

CHAPTER XIV — THE WORLD SECURITY COMMITTEE

THE TRANSFORMATION HAD STARTED TO EXTEND to all parts of Africa. The news of the transformation first spread throughout the surrounding villages and soon made its way across the nation. Media outlets had begun to report a strange lack of patients in hospitals and a subsiding of violence in communities where police were no longer being run off their feet. But the mainstream media insisted this was nothing more than an awful trick. According to these conformists, the glorious civilisations that humans had built over thousands of years were now facing the threat of destruction. The threat had been named the "Dreadful Collapse".

This perspective ran parallel to the World Security Committee's view. Though the Committee looked very political, it was actually made up of many international corporations with interests in everything from insurance and finance, to medicine and food.

The Security Committee proclaimed that the world was facing a wolf in sheep's clothing. They assured the global population that the reason the enemy had been allowed to pass through without police or military opposition was because it was a necessary ploy in the governments' grand plan of retaliation. Without the national guards, they would easily take over.

Unfortunately, the media companies that disagreed with the Committee were scarce in number, and the mainstream media were having greater power of influence over the people. They continued to plant seeds of hate and resentment against the Guvernians in the minds of people. In fact, news broke that people who believed in the hope offered by the Guvernians were being prosecuted. Despite the continent of Africa, which was now experiencing peace and happiness for the first time in centuries, widespread chaos and confusion raged throughout the world. The World Security Committee kept a careful eye on those who supported the Guvernian invasion. Professor Albert Smith was one of the people on the Committee's watch list. He was considered an expert in the field of DNA, and his knowledge of recent discoveries was considered a threat.

The Committee was working hard to find any weaknesses of their enemy, which was proving difficult after the discovery of their immortality. The premise of their retaliation was their enemy threatened the world order and humankind's dominion, and it simply could not be allowed. They could not make negotiations with the enemy. They had seen for themselves the capabilities of the Guvernians—their ability to hypnotise armies and render them useless. General Watson had been invited to join the World Security Committee because his experience would prove invaluable.

One day before joining this meeting, the General had moved the National Security's camp in the desert to another area. The reason for this was because the Guvernians had come too close to their area.

The General, along with soldiers from the World Security Committee, would now lead operations from a second aircraft-carrier in the Mediterranean, tasked to the WSC.

Two days before this change of position, Colonel Williams and his team had already left for the Quadronia Gate, not knowing what to expect. The General had not sent them to destroy the Quadronia Gate but to test the effectiveness of the prototype laser shields.

Colonel Williams and his team planned on making a surprise attack on the Quadronia Gate. They had moved south, making sure not to meet any Guvernians on the way.

The General demanded that the Colonel and his team stay in contact with him at all times. They were also instructed to keep their laser shields on, whether there were any Guvernians in the area or not. Lastly, they were not to get any closer to the Quadronia Gate than 5km. However, these warnings meant nothing more than maintaining a facade. The General had a greater intention. He knew the unit would never reach the area.

The Colonel commanded the soldier responsible for watching the radar, "Soldier, I want to know about everything that moves across that screen!"

Without lifting his head, the soldier responded, "Yes, Sir!"

All of the soldiers were on alert, even though the radar monitor showed the area to be clear. But they could all hear the distant galloping of horses.

The soldiers readied their weapons as the horses approached. The soldiers' shields did little to protect them as the entire area lit up, dropping the soldiers to the ground and transforming them.

The General watched the events unfold back at base camp, hands once again clenched into white fists. He felt his stomach twist in anxiousness.

***

Two days later, the General boarded an army plane to attend the World Security Committee meeting in Geneva.

The Committee cunningly thought that in order to gain public support, they would televise the General's address. When the General reached his podium, a great applause exploded.

"Esteemed members of the World Security Committee," the General started. "It is a great honour for me to be here at a time like this. Unfortunately, our world is facing its greatest threat in the history of humanity. As you all know, the unrecognisable energy that was released after the earthquake in Africa has opened a door to this foreign civilisation. We sent a well-equipped team to the area to assess the severity of the threat, and if appropriate, destroy it. But our enemies moved quickly and rendered our teams ineffective."

"According to the intelligence I have received, we have two solutions and not a lot of time to act. The first of these is we have to close this evil gate immediately. According to our research, after strenuous testing, our scientists believe the energy that opened the Quadronia Gate was caused by the cracking of the earth's crust, forcing magma to the surface. If we can tap into a similar energy source, we may have a shot at closing the gate. We have only one option: create an artificial earthquake. Unfortunately, the only way to do this is with nuclear bombs. As we have seen previously, this will damage the soil and potentially cause deformations in the flora and fauna. But we must take the risk for the greater good."

"...We have only one option: create an artificial earthquake. Unfortunately, the only way to do this is with nuclear bombs.."

As the General said this, another explosion of applause resounded throughout the room.

Reassured by the applause, the General continued his speech in an active tone:

"The second thing we have to do is to find a way to protect ourselves from the enemy's weapons. As you also know, the weapons are biological in nature. The enemy seems to emit hypnotising light from their eyes. The army had designed shields that we hoped would protect us from their laser light. Unfortunately, they were unsuccessful. If we can't find a solution to this..." he paused to allow himself, and his audience, to embrace the emotion of the moment. He continued, "For centuries, we have overcome many obstacles. We will fight and we will be victorious."

Then, after wiping his nose, he continued:

"Humanity is not weak and desperate. History shows we have defeated many obstacles in our way. And the fact that we are still alive is great proof to this. We are going to fight, and like all previous obstacles, we are going to overcome this." Again the room was filled with thunderous applause. The General had given hope to the whole world that had been waiting in fear.

The General pressed on:

"The African continent must immediately shut down all connections with other continents in order to contain the invasion of our enemy. Many military units under the command of the World Security Committee have been placed at Gibraltar Strait in Spain, in the Red Sea, and in the Gulf of Suez in Egypt. I know that you honoured members are going to make the best decision. Thank you."

As he got down from the podium, the members of the World Security Committee stood up and applauded the General. With this, the General had received the permission he had needed to do what was necessary to stop this foreign threat to the entire planet.

GUVERNIA PARADISE

CHAPTER XV — ISLAND

WHEN JACK WAS ONLY SEVEN YEARS OLD, GRAHAM had taken his family on a vacation to the Californian coast. Graham watched as his son Jack ran along the beach, playing in the golden sand, giggling all the while. Jack was very happy, and this happiness reminded Graham of his own childhood.

"Dad, Dad! Look!" Jack yelled excitedly.

Graham looked at him with a big smile. "Come on, Jack! Faster! Faster!" he encouraged. Jack raced the waves that covered and erased the footprints that Jack made, and Jack ran forwards and backwards, trying to leave new prints.

The sound of the sea remained the same, but the images of his memory became weaker—fading until they disappeared. Captain Graham Lawrence Graham Lawrence squeezed his eyes shut, desperately wanting to relive the memory again. Suddenly, a sharp pain throughout his body brought him back to reality, and he opened his eyes.

Slightly confused, he thought he was back in California. He tried to call out to Jack but was paralysed.

The familiar images reappeared, this time feeling more real.

Caroline and Jack were calling out to him. "Come on Dad, hurry up! The picnic is ready!" his son shouted.

Graham looked at them and smiled. "Come on, Graham!" his wife beckoned. Caroline, in her ethereal white dress, resembled an angel.

Graham slowly started to approach them. But this time, a wave that had just rolled onto shore had washed over his face, tearing him away from the memory of the family he adored so much.

When he opened his eyes, he realised he was still lying on the ground.

Where am I? he thought.

The images of his memory became weaker—fading until they disappeared. Captain Graham Lawrence Graham Lawrence squeezed his eyes shut, desperately wanting to relive the memory again.

Suddenly, he remembered his ship capsizing, sinking slowly to the bottom of the sea. He tried to lift his head and take in his surroundings, but he was exhausted. He tried to pull himself up as best he could, but it took him a few attempts before he made it to a sitting position. He felt powerless and weak. When he looked at his surroundings, he saw an endless expanse of water. As he looked around and more things came into view, he realised he was on a small, isolated island. *Am I the only survivor?*

Weeks, months, and even years had passed. During the first days, at first, Graham had counted the days and months that passed, but keeping track of the time that he was separated from his family brought him unbearable pain.

He would often get lost in thought, gazing out at the ocean that stretched out infinitely. These waters separated him from his loved ones and seemed like the world's cruellest dungeon. It had mercilessly separated Graham from his wife and his only son. Some days, the pain became too much and Graham found himself angrily kicking the waters.

Suddenly, he remembered his ship capsizing, sinking slowly to the bottom of the sea. He tried to lift his head and take in his surroundings, but he was exhausted.

Sometimes, he thought this was divine judgement dealt upon him. In the past, he had taken for granted the preciousness of time. But the thing that gave him the most pain were those times he had put his job as a priority over the people he loved. Those times he wished he could just take back and use wisely.

"But, Dad, please..." Jack had begged. The words seem to ring in his ears, twisting into his heart like a dagger.

During the first days stranded on the island, Graham had spent most of his time on its summit, hoping to spot a rescue ship. But now he couldn't even remember if those days were real or just another dream. The days seemed to blur into one, making everything hazy.

Hope soon faded, and Captain Graham Lawrence was now left to feel only loneliness, regret, and a great deal of longing. This was the greatest punishment that anyone could bear.

GUVERNIA PARADISE

CHAPTER XVI — DREADFUL DECISION

THE WORLD SECURITY COMMITTEE ORGANISED A secret meeting, closed off from the press. The members had been called to the meeting by the emergency alarm. Immediate and drastic measures had to be implemented because the Guvernian invasion of the African continent had occurred at such a rapid rate. This had created great panic. The World Security Committee felt the planet slipping out of their control, and they remained adamant that was not going to happen. The Guvernians were now knocking on the doors of Europe and Asia, and who knew how much time they had left before reaching the rest of the world.

The General Secretary opened the meeting:

"Respected members of the Committee, as you already know, the rate at which our enemy has raided Africa has horrified the entire world. Satellite imagery shows that Africa now belongs to the Guvernians, no longer a part of the free world. As of today, our planet has been divided.

"The enemy has reached Morocco and, in a matter of time, it will reach the Gulf of Suez in Egypt. In a few short hours, our enemy will engage with our military units. We are still pushing our nuclear weapon options, but we understand this is not a popular course of action. However, they have been readied in case we decide to initialise them today."

"Solely out of interest," asked one of the attending members, "are you able to give us further details about the nuclear weapons?"

"The nuclear weapons will be used to create a high-magnitude earthquake, similar to the one that triggered the opening of the Quadronia Gate. We hope to harness the consequential energy to shut the gate the Guvernians have escaped through."

The Guvernians were now knocking on the doors of Europe and Asia, and who knew how much time they had left before reaching the rest of the world.

"Mr. Secretary," the same member replied, "how many nuclear weapons are at our disposal?"

"We have six nuclear warheads ready to launch," the General Secretary answered.

For a short time, silence rang out over the room, to be broken only by the bustle of nervous chatter. The tension in the room became palpable. Finally, the General Secretary intervened with a firm, confident voice: "Please, esteemed members! Please. We don't have another option. We must not waste anymore time arguing with one another. Every minute from now on is of critical importance if we wish to secure the future of our planet. The order of this wonderful world will either live on in triumph, or everything will be buried in darkness."

The General Secretary signalled for voting to take place. Many of the members looked to one another, unsure of what to do. But the same question pierced each of their minds: what if we completely destroy our world while trying to save it?

However, the Committee had a different agenda. Their main concern was not the well-being of the planet but rather their luxurious lifestyles. Kings seated on glorious thrones.

Africa had stopped selling and, therefore, buying medical supplies. If the Guvernians continued to spread across Earth, then medicine would no longer be sold or bought—at all. The pharmaceutical trade was the Committee's greatest source of income—revenue they could not afford to lose. If they were to lose it, they would most certainly lose their control over the world. For the sake of their wealth, for the sake of their power, they were willing to risk the lives of so many people.

The General Secretary knew that even though the members were uneasy about the vote, their decisions would be redundant. The result had been known since the very beginning. The respected members and the companies behind them had already made up their minds. This was never up for debate.

The General Secretary left the room and called General Watson to inform him of the decision.

"Yes, sir," General Watson said, smiling. "We are immediately starting the operation."

The General Secretary took a deep breath then looked at the world map hanging from his wall.

The Guvernians had already reached Morocco and, therefore, getting closer to the borders of Europe. The Guvernians saw the Gibraltar Strait and the many military ships put into position there. The ships, anchored at port, first heard a sound of a horn and then the coastal skies of Morocco started to clear. The Guvernians had arrived.

The sounding of the alarm from the ship was followed by an announcement.

"Put your earphones on and do not look at them! Turn your faces away at all times," the announcer warned.

In a great panic, the soldiers quickly put on their earphones and then turned away from the Guvernians. Their pulses started to race and their fear for the enemy immobilised them.

But they could not prepare for the Guvernian's horn, which had the power to turn ships towards them.

Eterno's song began to make its way into the minds of the soldiers, pulling them towards their freedom. It was irresistible to them.

General Watson watched on as the song affected a ship. "No, it can't be!" he shouted. "We are losing our European units!" The General unsuccessfully tried to make contact with the command centre of the ship.

"Clear the ant hole," the General shouted! He sent four cargo planes to follow his primary scouting warplanes. The fighter planes left the World Security Committee's aircraft-carrier, based in the Mediterranean, with coordinates for Africa.

The General made contact with the pilots via the intercom. "Keep your altitude!" he told them. "Your landing point has been determined. For the safety of your mission, the coordinates of this point will not be given to you. When you are fifty kilometres from your landing point, please set your plane on auto pilot, and we will take control from there."

"Yes, Sir," the pilots responded.

Jack, who was still travelling with the Guvernians, had reached the Red Sea. He realised by their unusually troubled faces that there was a problem.

"Is everything all right?" he asked, turning to Argen.

Jack had never seen Argen so quiet and thoughtful.

"The virus that rules humanity doesn't want to leave," Argen responded. "The people think this war is between us and them. They are wrong. The war is between humanity and people's ego. Jack, beyond these waters, comes a resistance."

"There is not much time left," Argen continued, looking into Jack's eyes. "I have to keep the promise I gave you. I have to go."

"Where are you going?" Jack asked.

"The nuclear weapons will be used to create a high-magnitude earthquake, similar to the one that triggered the opening of the Quadronia Gate..."

"To find your dad. I have to bring Solare's light of life to him before it's too late."

Jack looked upon Argen with overwhelming emotion. He was so very thankful but sad to see his friend go.

Argen quickly jumped and dived into the waters and disappeared from sight.

"Goodbye, my friend," Jack said, with tears in his eyes.

GUVERNIA PARADISE

CHAPTER XVII — GREAT EXPLOSION

THE WORLD SECURITY COMMITTEE'S WARPLANES and cargo planes, which carried the devastatingly powerful nuclear weapons, landed south of the Quadronia Gate.

Military units transported their equipment five kilometres north to where they set up camp and began work immediately. They had been ordered to drill 600 metres into the ground and to lower the warheads down the shafts with mobile elevators.

The warheads could be controlled from the command centre only. The General did not trust anyone else to do it. He ensured that a live feed was set up to broadcast the mission to base camp, so he could keep a close eye on what was happening. As soon as the bombs were in position and switched to stand-by mode, the shafts were sealed shut with cement-like chemicals in an effort to contain the blast.

The whole team was tense as the bombs were slowly and carefully lowered down the elevator shaft. Everyone knew how dangerous these bombs were, and a sense of unease settled over the camp.

"Be careful!" the Commander bellowed as one of the soldier's feet slipped and the bomb almost tumbled to the ground. They worked in silence, cold sweat dripping down their faces, hands shaking uncontrollably.

As soon as the bombs were in position and switched to stand-by mode, the shafts were sealed shut with cement-like chemicals in an effort to contain the blast.

The soldiers knew it was unethical for them to take such drastic measures. A voice in the backs of their minds kept niggling at them, reminding them of the seriousness of their actions. They weren't sure whether the voice came from their consciences or somewhere else.

When all of the bombs had been lowered safely, the Commander called the General.

"Sir, all the bombs have been positioned as ordered," he said.

"Good," he replied, sighing with relief. He was worried that the Guvernians would come across the operation.

"I'm going to activate the bombs. Make sure everyone is prepared."

"Yes, Sir," the officer replied.

"Soldier, it is in our nature to give and take orders. It makes us human and keeps things the way they should be. Do you understand?"

Although the soldier did not really understand, he knew how he was supposed to respond to his superior.

"Of course, Sir," nodding as he had been groomed to do so.

"Close the hole now!" the General ordered. "You have twenty minutes to leave the area! Go, go, go!"

"Yes, Sir!" the officer gave him a salute and turned on his heels.

The soldiers sealed the shafts shut. The cement-like chemical took immediate effect.

The General was smiling and speaking on the phone: "Sir, everything's done. In about twenty minutes, the bombs will set off an earthquake in Africa with the epicentre in the Sahara. After this, our world and humanity will be set free. Hooray to our world and our civilisations!" the General concluded.

The soldiers knew it was unethical for them to take such drastic measures. A voice in the backs of their minds kept niggling at them, reminding them of the seriousness of their actions.

He then praised his soldier, "You should be proud of yourself, soldier. You have shown great honour."

"Thank you, Sir. Thank you."

GUVERNIA PARADISE

CHAPTER XVIII — THE CLOSING OF THE QUADRONIA GATE

CAPTAIN GRAHAM LAWRENCE SALTED THE FISH HE had caught a short time earlier. He eagerly waited for the fish to finish cooking over the open fire. The familiar smell and taste of the fish allowed Graham to relive some pleasant memories, particularly that of a romantic evening when he and Caroline had eaten at a seafood restaurant. There was not often a reason to smile on the desolate island. Graham didn't want to open his eyes. He wanted more than anything to escape his depressing reality.

Then Graham heard someone call his name. First, he thought it was just his imagination. "Graham!" the voice called once more. When he turned around, he saw a child standing on the sand.

Graham rubbed his eyes, thinking he was seeing things. But the child with his smiling sweet face was still there.

With that sweet, comforting voice, he said, "My name is Argen. Jack sent me here."

Before he could respond, Argen's eyes lit up and the light washed over Graham. He felt strangely at peace. He had been transformed.

"I have to go now," Argen said. Graham smiled with his new Guvernian expression.

Argen dived back into the ocean and then disappeared into its depths.

***

The seconds were passing painstakingly slow. The General was bewitched with anger. With two minutes left before the nuclear weapons detonated, the General's throat started to tighten.

"Sir! The weapons have successfully detonated." The ancient African continent shook with deep groans, but this physical tremor was nothing compared to the emotional aggravation that took place in the Guvernians hearts.

For the first time in their lives, the Guvernians experienced what pain was. Pearl-like tears began to well up and drip onto their cheeks, their hearts broken.

Jack was still in the Suez, but immediately after the explosion, the Guvernians were yanked back towards the

Quadronia Gate. Solare was calling them back to their safe haven, free from the suffering of this hell.

Jack was shaken from his blissful dream by the explosion and found himself on the shores of the Red Sea. Everything seemed bleak and grey, and he was left with nothing but a bitter feeling in the pit of his stomach.

Ordion stood right beside the Quadronia Gate, helping the remaining Guvernians pass through safely.

One of the last people to arrive back at the gate was young Argen, who suddenly stopped in front of the gate and stood there wishing he didn't have to leave Jack. For the first time, he was experiencing a dilemma. His face was pale, and he looked worried. Argen pitied the dying, grey world with his shining blue eyes, wanting to illuminate the world one last time. Instead of passing through the Quadronia Gate, he turned abruptly from his Guvernian homeland and ran in the opposite direction.

"Argen!" Ordion called with a voice so powerful, it shook Earth.

Argen did not respond. He ran as fast as he could to where he left Jack. He couldn't leave his friend behind. It was then that Solare's wings of light were gifted to Argen.

He had to save Jack from the hands of a corrupt world. While the other Guvernians looked at him in shock and admiration, Argen rose gloriously with his golden wings. Flying came naturally to him.

He swiftly flew over to Jack, wings glinting in the sun. Jack squinted, trying to see what the speck of light approaching him was. At first, Jack couldn't look at the star-like speck hurtling above him, but then he recognised the sound that came from the light. It was the most beautiful sound he had ever heard.

Argen hooked Jack under his arms. Since Solare had decided Jack could live in Guvernia, Argen carried away his friend through the gate.

The Quadronia Gate rose steadily into the sky. It then disappeared like a shooting star.

GUVERNIA PARADISE

ABOUT THE AUTHOR

ISMAIL SERINKEN WAS BORN IN Weinheim, Germany, in 1971. He graduated with a degree in Korean Language and Literature. His first book, *Talking With God on the Way Back Home,* was made into a movie. He is a translator, television programer, and international speaker. He is married and lives in Ankara, Turkey, with his wife and three children.